HOLIDAY HOPES

When Lila Caswell travels from her Nashville home to London on business over Christmas, she decides to catch up over the phone with the Cornish family of her friend Belle, who died three years ago — which results in an unexpected invitation to come spend the holiday with them. There Lila meets Belle's widower Grant, and they are instantly attracted to each other. But grief for Belle still haunts them both. Lila blames herself for her friend's death. And is Grant ready to start a new relationship?

Books by Angela Britnell
in the Linford Romance Library:

HUSHED WORDS
FLAMES THAT MELT
SICILIAN ESCAPE
CALIFORNIA DREAMING
A SMOKY MOUNTAIN CHRISTMAS
ENDLESS LOVE
HOME AT LAST
AN UNEXPECTED LOVE
WHERE WE BELONG
WISHES CAN COME TRUE

ANGELA BRITNELL

HOLIDAY HOPES

Complete and Unabridged

LINFORD
Leicester

First published in Great Britain in 2016

First Linford Edition
published 2018

A catalogue record for this book is available
from the British Library.

ISBN 978–1–4448–3650–9

Published by
F. A. Thorpe (Publishing)
Anstey, Leicestershire

Set by Words & Graphics Ltd.
Anstey, Leicestershire
Printed and bound in Great Britain by
T. J. International Ltd., Padstow, Cornwall

This book is printed on acid-free paper

1

'You have to come,' Nick urged. 'I'm not taking no for an answer. What kind of mate would I be if I left you here in London alone for Christmas?'

A thoughtful one. Grant didn't speak his thoughts out loud, but his friend's expression darkened. They both knew why he didn't 'do' the holiday season or Cornwall anymore.

'It'll be a full house, but Mum's putting you out in the cottage,' Nick pleaded. 'You'll have privacy if we all get too much for you.' Grant hated being tiptoed around as though he might blow up. 'I'm going down a few days before Christmas and staying all the way through the New Year, but you don't have to do the same.'

Without being rude, he couldn't see any way out of agreeing to his worst nightmare — returning to the spot where his life fell apart and at a time of year when everyone else would be full of the spirit of love and goodwill. *Like that even exists.*

'I'm not dense, mate. I wouldn't have asked, but Mum really wants to see you.' Nick faltered and glanced away, staring down at the floor. 'You're not the only one who misses her. Sometimes I think you forget Belle was my sister.'

A painful surge of emotion tightened Grant's throat. 'No, I don't.' His clipped tones made Nick stare. 'Never. I never forget.'

'Sorry, I didn't mean to . . . '

'I know.' He sighed and shoved a hand up through his unruly hair. The dark shaggy curls desperately needed a good cut; something else he'd neglected.

'Last Christmas was the first year Mum could bear to put the tree up again. We're trying.'

And I'm not. I get it. He'd heard everyone's platitudes too many times — *it's been three years, you're young,* and the most cutting of all, that Belle

2

would want him to be happy again. How could anyone know that?

Grant didn't have the energy to argue any longer. 'Fine. I'll come.'

'You won't regret it.'

Yes, I probably will. He dragged out a half-smile and succumbed to his fate.

* * *

'Wow! This sure is pretty.' Lila craned her neck to stare out of the window as the taxi drove slowly along the narrow cobblestoned street. Festive multicoloured lights sparkled in the late-afternoon sunshine and danced over the flock of small fishing boats crowding the tiny harbour. 'I'm guessing we're not likely to get a white Christmas.'

'Shouldn't think so, my dear,' he chuckled. 'What's it like where you come from?'

Lila shrugged. 'Nashville's unpredictable. I've known it to be so warm and sunny that my brothers played basketball outside, or knee-deep in snow.'

'We'll be at Mendelby House in a few minutes. I didn't know the Warrens had any relatives in America,' he probed.

'I'm not a relation. Belle Warren and I were good friends.' Her voice faltered trying to talk about the girl who'd befriended her when she first came to England. They'd shared a flat when Lila was doing a three-month temporary placement at the London office of the cosmetics company she worked for. 'She often invited me here to visit her family, but I wasn't able to come before now.'

'That were a sad thing for them to lose her that way. Real tragedy. Pretty girl too, and nice with it.' The driver shook his head sadly.

The last thing she wanted was to discuss Belle. Over the last three years, she'd been in England many times on business, but purposely avoided getting in touch with the Warrens. She'd have been wise to do the same on this occasion, but instead she'd phoned Belle's mother to see how they were

4

doing. When Edith discovered that Lila wasn't returning to Nashville for the holidays, she'd insisted on her spending Christmas and New Year with them in Cornwall. The question weighing on her mind revolved around whether she'd have the nerve to talk to them about her guilt over Belle's death.

'Here you be.'

The car stopped outside an imposing granite house. Its solid facade faced the sea, and the white paint showed signs of being weathered by constant exposure to the wind and salt air. Before she could change her mind and consider asking the taxi driver to take her back to the train station, the front door opened. A woman stepped out, and Lila's breath caught in her throat. An older, grey-haired version of Belle greeted her with a broad smile, lighting up the same shade of bright blue eyes Lila remembered so well.

'That'll be fifteen pounds, my 'and-some.'

Lila mentally shook herself and paid

the driver, then lifted out her small suitcase from the car and carried it up the path.

'We're some pleased you've come, my dear. It'll be lovely to have the old house full again.' A shadow flitted across Edith Warren's face. 'Did I tell you our Nick's coming tomorrow? I can't remember if you met him.'

'Um, no, I didn't.' Belle had often talked about her older brother, but their paths never crossed during her short time in London.

'And we've got another visitor arriving on Wednesday.' Edith beamed. Lila's fantasy of a quiet week spent talking to Belle's parents and exploring the local area faded away. 'Grant Hawkins is coming. Belle's husband.'

Lila's stomach churned. Of all the people on the planet, he was the last person she wanted to spend Christmas with.

'Nick found out he didn't have any plans for the holidays and persuaded him to join us.' Her eyes dulled. 'He's stayed away too long, and I've missed the dear boy. I suppose he couldn't face us.'

I can't face him either.

'We were all disappointed when you couldn't make it to their wedding. How's your grandmother doing now?'

'She's good, thanks. I hated to let Belle down, but I couldn't leave Nashville when she was so ill.' Lila wasn't around for Belle's whirlwind romance with Grant. Belle knew him as her brother's friend for years but all of a sudden when they met again it'd turned into something far more. The constant stream of emails, text messages and Facebook posts crossing the Atlantic between the two women meant Lila wasn't surprised by the couple's quick engagement.

Edith straightened her shoulders, and a flash of the same quiet strength that'd underpinned Belle's ebullient character shone through.

'We're determined to have a good Christmas. It was Belle's favourite holiday and she'd hate to see us moping. I'm planning to give Grant a good talking-to while he's here, because Nick says he's buried himself in work and never goes out. It's not right.' She gave Lila a shrewd stare. 'You can help and back me up.'

Talking to Grant about his late wife was the stuff of Lila's nightmares and wouldn't happen if she could help it. She plastered on a bright smile and prepared to lie. 'Of course.' If Grant intended to stay long, it wouldn't be hard to arrange a sudden need for her to leave as soon as Christmas was over. She only hoped that would be soon enough.

2

Grant randomly tossed clothes into a small bag and got ready to leave. He'd avoided driving down to Cornwall with Nick earlier in the week by insisting he couldn't leave until the twenty-third because of having too much work. His friend tactfully didn't call him out on the obvious lie.

He'd made an attempt to go back to teaching after losing Belle, but after a tough six months gave it up as a bad idea. At first he picked up any odd jobs to pay the bills, but then rediscovered his love of carpentry, something he'd learnt from his father as a young boy. Grant found that the soothing aspect of making something with his hands took the edge off of the bitterness weighing him down. Now he had his own small business and made enough money to fund his stripped-down lifestyle. He'd sold the beautiful home he'd shared with Belle and bought a half-derelict terraced house on the outskirts of Watford. All his free time was spent bringing the house back to life, with the added bonus of helping himself out along the way.

Grant took the stairs two at a time and hurried out of the front door. He'd sold the flashy sports car he'd bought when he got his doctorate, so he'd be taking the train down to Cornwall. The car had been an extravagance he couldn't afford to keep, but the main reason for getting rid of it was the undeniable association with Belle. She'd loved nothing better than taking a long ride on a sunny day with her long blonde hair blowing in the wind as she laughed and urged him to put his foot down and go faster.

A shard of grief pierced through him and Grant forced himself to keep walking. A quick twenty-minute ride from the bus stop down the road would get him into Paddington Station. He'd arrive in Truro around half past four this afternoon, and Nick would pick him up.

Already the idea of facing Belle's parents again made him nauseous. They hadn't met since her funeral, and he'd even put them off coming to the house afterwards to sort through her things. Instead he'd boxed everything up and sent it all to Cornwall without keeping anything for himself. In the short, brittle conversation he'd had with Edith, the poor woman hadn't been able to understand why he didn't need a collection of Belle's dresses, jewellery or shoes to remind him of her daughter.

Grant hopped onto the bus and lowered himself into a seat, tucking his long legs out of the way and closing his eyes.

* * *

'Would you like to ride into Truro with Nick later on to pick up Grant?' Edith asked. 'It's a pretty town and it'll be right busy today. They've got the best Christmas decorations and lights in the whole of Cornwall.'

Lila speared her last delicious bite of homemade quiche while deciding on the best way to refuse the kind offer. The two women were on their own for lunch because Mr. Warren was working in the family's hardware shop and Nick had gone to meet a few old friends at the pub. 'That's sweet of you, but I've got presents to wrap, and I might even take a nap after my long walk this morning.'

'That's a shame. Nick would enjoy your company.'

Be a little bit more subtle, please. Ever since he arrived on Tuesday, it'd been obvious the direction Edith's mind was taking. The combination of one adored single son and one reasonably attractive single woman meant only one thing in Edith Warren's book. Lila didn't have the heart to tell her she was wasting her time. For one thing, she wouldn't be here long enough to kick start any romance, and the second problem was Nick himself. His regular good looks and pleasant manners weren't unappealing, but his startling resemblance to Belle from the vivid blue eyes to his wavy blond hair unsettled her. If she'd done things differently three years ago, Belle might be alive today.

'I expect he'll survive,' she said with a lightness she didn't feel. 'Can I do the dishes or help you get ready for dinner tonight? I'm pretty handy in the kitchen.'

'I'm all right, my 'andsome. Later maybe. You run along.'

She made her escape, and up in her tiny attic room Lila quickly wrapped the few presents she'd brought from London — perfume for Edith and Tennessee whisky for the men; luckily she'd packed extra of each just in case. She kicked off her shoes to lie on the bed and tucked a pillow behind her head. Half an hour later she abandoned trying to get off to sleep and picked up her phone. She scrolled through until she found the wedding pictures Belle sent when she was forced to miss the big day.

It wasn't hard to see why Belle fell head over heels for the handsome history professor. Love shone from his sparkling green eyes as they rested on his beautiful bride, and his arm protectively circled her slim waist. His tall, broad frame nicely filled out what Belle had explained to Lila was called a morning suit. Not every man could carry off the dark tail coat, fine pinstripe trousers, white shirt, grey waistcoat and grey silk tie — not forgetting the grey top hat he carried in his hand. But Grant Hawkins did, and with style.

Lila sighed and set the phone back down on the bedside table. She'd get through Christmas somehow and flee back to London on Monday. *You know things are never that simple.*

'Lila. The boys are back and I've made us all a cup of tea.' Edith's voice penetrated her consciousness and she startled, jerking up in the bed and staring at the antique silver travel clock she never left home without. She

14

must've drifted off after all, because it was five o'clock already.

'I'll be down in a minute,' she shouted, and hurried to the bathroom. Lila delved into her make-up bag and dug out a new bright red lipstick to add a touch of colour to her pale features. She didn't have time to fiddle with her mussed-up hair, so pulled it back into her usual ponytail before adding a scarlet ribbon for a festive touch. The dark jeans and red jumper she'd worn all day would have to do.

For a moment she hesitated before opening her bedroom door and heading down the stairs. Voices drifted out into the hall, and the new, deeper one added to the mix made her stomach churn. Lila took a deep breath and stepped into the kitchen.

Grant registered two things in the time it took him to stand up. First, the woman staring at him was stunning. Absolutely drop-dead gorgeous. From her glossy ebony hair, caught up with a red ribbon, to her wide, generous mouth, everything about Lila Caswell was vibrant and bursting with life. But the second was her obvious shock at his haggard appearance. He supposed she'd only have seen pictures of him on his wedding day, and since then grief had stripped him to the bone.

As they shook hands, her observant hazel eyes, flecked with bright shards of gold and framed with long dark lashes, swept down over him.

'It's a pleasure to meet you, Belle . . .' His voice hitched but he ploughed on. 'She always spoke fondly of you.' When Nick said the American woman would be spending Christmas with them as well, it'd been disconcerting. Things were bad enough already without adding another layer of tension to his visit. Grant didn't know what to say when she stood there speechless, and could've kissed Nick's mother when she bustled back into the kitchen.

Edith smiled around the room. 'I'm going to cut the Christmas cake to have with our tea.' She gestured towards the chair next to Grant. 'Sit down, Lila. You two can have a good natter.'

A flash of panic lit up Lila's eyes, and he guessed it stemmed from the same emotions he'd faced so many times since losing Belle. More than once he'd watched old friends cross the street because they didn't know what to say to him, not realising he didn't need eloquent sympathy, only a simple acknowledgement of his grief. Meeting Edith again a few minutes ago was as awful as he'd expected. They'd silently clung to each other, and when she finally let go of him she only stared and shook her head, her quiet gesture speaking volumes.

'If you'll forgive me, I'm going to give tea a miss.' Grant forced himself to smile. 'I already had some on the train and I'd like to get unpacked.'

Edith patted his arm. 'Of course, love. I've put you out in the cottage, but . . . ' Her voice trailed away. *Maybe I shouldn't have put you there because it'll bring back too many memories. But*

I didn't think you'd want to be in the house with us all and I wasn't sure what to do for the best. He understood her unspoken words only too well. This wasn't easy for any of them.

'That's fine, honestly,' Grant tried to reassure her. 'Excuse me, Lila. I'll see you all at dinner later.' Before anyone could stop him, he picked up his bag from the floor and headed for the back door. The second he stepped outside, a crushing memory of the first time he came here with Belle swept over him. She'd laughed as he swung her into his arms and carried her all the way up the narrow path to the tiny cottage, built at the back of the property years earlier for a son who'd never married and wasn't capable of living independently. He could either fight against the recollections or deal with them, and it was long past time to do the latter.

His good intentions lasted until he turned the old-fashioned brass key in the lock and opened the front door. The sight of the well-worn red leather sofa where he'd deposited a giggling Belle before kissing her senseless undid him. Grant dropped his bag, covered his face with his hands and wept.

How he'd get through the weekend, he didn't have a clue.

3

'Poor boy. It's been hard on him.' Edith's eyes glazed over with unshed tears.

If Lila thought she'd known guilt before she came to Cornwall, it was nothing in comparison to this. She nodded but didn't attempt to speak, because her voice appeared to have deserted her.

'Mum, I'll put the kettle on. You get the cake.' Nick's assertive tone surprised Lila. 'I hear Dad's car outside.' The hint of warning in his words said Mr. Warren wouldn't want to walk in and find his family miserable.

'That's a good idea,' Edith declared. 'Lila will wish she hadn't come in a minute.'

'Not at all. I love it here.' Apart from Grant turning up today and upsetting her equilibrium, she'd totally fallen in love with Cornwall. She'd made the most of the last couple of days and enjoyed the mild, dry weather. Port Carne itself was everything she'd expected, at least to an addict of Doc Martin, with its eerie resemblance to the fictional Port Wenn. She'd taken a long walk each day over the nearby cliffs to fuel her Poldark fantasies, trawled through the local shops and indulged in more than one delicious pasty.

Edith opened a big square tin and carefully took out a large cake covered in white icing and decorated with a variety of small plastic Christmas figures. 'I bet you've never seen one of these before.' She set it down on a pretty china plate and picked up a silver cake knife. 'Do you like fruit cake?'

Um, no, it's disgusting. Lila's good manners, drummed into her by her mother, wouldn't allow her to be rude. 'I expect yours are very different.' Her evasive answer appeared to satisfy Edith, who smiled and proceeded to cut a large slice and slip it onto a plate. 'There you go.' She pushed it across the table in her direction.

'Tell me about the recipe. I've never seen anything like this before.' Lila played for time. She listened in fascination as Belle's mother told her about the rich fruit cake she'd made several months ago and laced with brandy at weekly intervals ever since. 'What's the yellow layer?'

'Marzipan. I put that on a couple of weeks ago and let it dry before I did the icing.'

Lila gingerly broke off a piece. 'Oh, the icing is hard.'

'It's royal icing. That's traditional, although these days some people use that fondant stuff.' Edith turned up her nose.

Lila took a bite, relieved to see none of the large glacé fruits she hated in the American version. 'Oh my God, it's delicious,' she laughed. 'Where I come from, fruit cakes are the most dreaded Christmas presents. People often re-gift them or throw them away. Now I realise it's because we don't know how to make a good one.'

Edith beamed. 'I'm some glad you like it. Nick, pour the tea.' He gave Lila an appreciative nod behind his mother's back.

'Have you cut the Christmas cake without me? You bad-mannered rabble,' John Warren said as he breezed in, kissed his wife and grabbed a slice of cake from the plate. He took the mug Nick held out and swigged a mouthful of tea before taking a large bite of cake. 'Another good one. No one can match your recipe.'

'I hope you had success out shopping. Nick told me you sneaked out for a while this afternoon while he watched the shop,' Edith probed, and John laughingly told her to mind her own business. Something about the couple's warm exchange got to Lila, and she blinked back tears.

Nick rested his warm hand on her shoulder. 'Homesick?' he murmured.

'A little.'

He glanced at his watch. 'The local

choir will be singing carols down on the quay soon. Would you like to come with me and hear them?'

'I'd love to.'

'Why don't you ask Grant to join you?' Edith suggested. 'It'd do him good to get out.'

'I'll ask, but I'm pretty sure he'll say no.'

'Do you want me to try?' The question popped out before Lila could stop to think of the possible consequences.

'If you like.' Nick sounded surprised and she couldn't blame him. 'The concert starts at seven, and we ought to get there around half past six to guarantee a decent spot.'

'I'm sure I can persuade him.' Lila headed for the kitchen door and struggled to ignore the butterflies fighting a war in her stomach.

Grant considered ignoring the loud knocking because he'd no doubt Edith had sent Nick to check on him. He dragged himself off the sofa to open the door. 'I should've guessed . . . ' He

24

stumbled over his words. 'Oh, I didn't expect it to be you. Sorry, I didn't mean . . . '

'Quit apologising. Can I come in?' Lila didn't wait for a reply and stepped around him. 'Nick and I are goin' to walk into the village to listen to the local choir singing carols down by the harbour. We're leaving in about twenty minutes and thought you'd like to join us.'

On what planet did that enter your heads?

'I'm sure you don't want to, but it won't kill you to make an effort for Edith's sake. She's fretting about you.'

He pulled himself out of simply listening to her low, honeyed drawl and realised he was being berated. In a quasi-polite way, she'd called him self-ish. 'Fine.'

'You'll come?' Her voice rose in a squeak.

Grant guessed she hadn't expected him to say yes and got a kick from catching her out. 'Unless you're retracting the invitation?'

'Certainly not,' she retorted. 'You might want to shave and change into some decent clothes.'

'I could've sworn you mentioned carol singing, not a fashion show.'

'Do you want to let the Warrens down?'

'I've already done that.'

The ticking clock on the mantelpiece reverberated in the silence hanging between them.

'Now it's my turn to be sorry,' Lila said quietly. 'I can be pushy sometimes.'

Grant gave her a wry smile. 'You think?'

'It's been said before,' she conceded.

'I can't imagine why.'

Lila's chin tilted. 'So, are you coming or not?'

This must be how she wore people down. He gave in and nodded.

'Good. We'll see you in . . . ' She glanced at her watch. ' . . . eighteen minutes.'

He almost asked what his punishment would be for being late, but kept his mouth shut because she'd only twist his words again.

Lila suppressed the urge to run back to the house in case he was watching. She couldn't believe she'd been so outspoken. *Some would call you rude and mouthy.* An ex-boyfriend's words came back to haunt her. The problem was, it'd been either that or try to comfort Grant, and too much sympathy on her part could lead them into dangerous territory.

Grief had worn Grant down, eroded the soft edges and left behind a hard-featured man, careless of his appearance and preferring his own company.

It's partly your fault. Do you think by making him listen to a few carols, that'll make up for the action you should've taken three years ago?

Lila mentally shook herself. She refused to ruin Christmas this way if only for Belle's sake. Her friend adored the holidays and always started playing carols in November before decorating every inch of space in their tiny flat. Lila forced a smile and walked back into the kitchen. 'Mission accomplished.'

Nick's eyebrows rose. 'Seriously? What on earth did you do to convince him?'

You don't want to know. It was borderline unkind. 'I simply evoked the spirit of Christmas and appealed to his good nature.'

Edith beamed at Lila. 'Oh, I'm some pleased.'

'You'll need a coat. It'll be chilly down on the quay, but at least it's not raining for once,' Nick commented.

'I'll go and get one. I need to change my shoes too.' She ran up to her room and stood for a moment, resting her shaking hands on top of the dressing table in an effort to calm down. Her mother always complained that Lila ploughed into things without thinking first, but this time she couldn't afford to keep doing that or people would be hurt — including her.

Lila quietly got ready, swapping her thin flat shoes for the pair of smart black leather boots she'd treated herself to before leaving Nashville. She slipped her short black wool coat back on and knotted a soft red mohair scarf around her neck. With her lipstick redone, and carrying a red hat and gloves to pop on when they got outside, Lila hummed to herself as she hurried back downstairs. She ground to a halt in the hall and tried not to stare.

'Do I pass inspection?' Grant challenged her, and for a moment she couldn't speak. Drops of water caught the light from where he'd attempted to tame his mass of dark unruly curls, and his clean-shaven jaw showed signs of irritation. But it was his eyes that drew her attention, because they'd acquired hints of bright green along with a faint trace of amusement. He'd abandoned the scruffy jeans and faded black T-shirt, replacing them with a pair of smart grey trousers, a dark blue brushed cotton shirt and a buttery soft black leather jacket.

'I guess you'll do.' Lila prayed he didn't pick up on the tremor in her voice.

'Don't overdo it now.'

'I won't. It's not good for you,' she quipped. Out of the corner of her eye, she noticed Nick glancing between the two of them with a puzzled expression. 'Come on, gentlemen, let's find out if either of you can sing!'

4

Grant struggled to ignore the drift of lemony perfume teasing his senses, but it wasn't easy with Lila plastered up against his side. She'd determinedly slipped a hand through his and Nick's arms as they walked down the steep hill towards the village. He was glad for the cover of darkness, only relieved by the night stars and an occasional street-light.

'Y'all don't go in for outside Christmas lights and stuff, do you?' Lila laughed. 'Heck, if you walked around any neighbourhood near me, you'd see inflatable snowmen, plastic reindeers on the rooftops, and more lights than you can shake a stick at.'

'We tend to keep most of our decorations inside,' Nick said with a slight hint of disapproval.

'Belle didn't,' Grant commented

31

before he could help himself. 'I've never known anybody to love Christmas more.' He launched into the story of their first Christmas together, when she'd almost bankrupted them by buying every decoration she could lay her hands on. She'd made him string coloured lights all over the front of their house — she didn't do white and tasteful and laughed with exuberant glee when he turned them on with a flourish.

'That's a lovely memory.' Lila's quiet words touched him, and for the first time he could agree. 'I remember her transforming our tiny flat into a regular Santa's grotto.'

'I'm sure.' Grant cracked a proper smile.

'We usually stand over there by the ice-cream shop.' Nick pointed to the far side of the quay. 'Hopefully we're early enough.' He forged ahead, greeting people he knew as he wended through the growing crowd.

Grant dropped behind with Lila, and

a curl of pleasure sneaked through him as she tightened her hold on his arm. His ricocheting emotions confused him. One minute thoughts of Belle threatened to swamp him, and the next he couldn't stop sneaking glances at the attractive woman by his side.

'It's messing with me too, if that's any help,' Lila whispered.

'What are you talking about?' He struggled to act confused by her question, but one quizzical raise of her eyebrows told him he'd been rumbled. 'We'd better join Nick.'

'Yeah, we certainly had.'

Flirting wasn't part of his agenda, so why was he disappointed that Lila didn't want to continue their conversation?

'This is so beautiful.' Lila smiled and gazed around, forcing him to pay attention. The choir, all bundled up in their winter coats and laughing and chatting away happily, stood in front of the wall in a semicircle. A small brass band off to one side tuned their instruments and got ready to play. Christmas lights twinkled all around the harbour, swaying in the slight breeze blowing in off of the sea, and their reflections skittered across the dark still water. The brightly coloured fishing boats were all tied up for the holidays. 'I could get used to this.'

'I suppose you'll be heading back to Nashville soon?'

'Not for a few weeks.'

'Really?'

'Pleased or disappointed?' A rush of heat coloured her cheeks, and Grant guessed she'd take the question back if she could.

'What are you two talking about?' Nick asked, and Grant felt guilty for ignoring his old friend. Their long history went back to their university days when they bonded over a mutual hatred of an arrogant philosophy professor. When Nick discovered Grant had no family apart from his father, who he rarely saw, he'd insisted on them travelling to Cornwall together for

Christmas. Belle, only sixteen then and already stunning, bewitched Grant's shy nineteen-year-old self and tongue tied-him so he could barely speak. He'd never forgotten her, but it'd been five years before they met again. Nick invited Belle to a birthday party at their London flat, and the lightning bolt struck them both hard. Six months later, they'd walked down the aisle, and Grant knew himself to be the luckiest man on earth.

'Nothing important.' He didn't dare look at Lila. 'Good crowd tonight.' During his brief marriage, they'd spent every Christmas here in the same guest cottage where he now slept alone. Belle loved this annual carol singing, and her tuneful soprano always rang out pitch-perfect. Grant unthinkingly grasped Lila's arm.

'It helps that it's not blowing a gale and lashing rain tonight,' Nick laughed.

The first notes of 'Hark the Herald Angels Sing' rang out and the choir started to sing, their harmonious voices soaring to the sky. None of the people watching needed any song sheets, and soon everyone began to join in. Grant surprised himself by doing the same, and put it down as an automatic reaction; certainly nothing to do with the unaccustomed lightness of spirit infecting him tonight.

Lila sang along, but her awareness zeroed in on Grant's solid warmth next to her and the sound of his deep melodic voice. She'd take a wild guess this was the first time he'd sung any Christmas carols since losing Belle. Maybe in her own small way she'd helped his thawing process, but still an uncomfortable chill trickled through her. The fragile thread of connection they'd formed would be blown apart if he ever found out she might've been able to save his wife.

'Thank you,' he whispered as the music stopped and everyone started to clap.

'What for?'

'All of this.' Grant gestured around

them. 'You might be a bully, but you did it for the best of reasons.'

Lila swallowed hard. The choir started to sing the next carol and the special moment between them receded. Finally the conductor announced the last song, and a lone trumpeter played the first notes of 'Silent Night' before the choir began to join in.

Lila's breath caught in a sob, and Grant wrapped his hand around hers. 'This one always gets to me too,' he murmured.

'At the late Christmas Eve service back home, a wonderful tenor always performs it as a solo before we all light candles and walk out in silence.'

'They do a similar thing here tomorrow. Would you like to go?' Grant asked. 'I will if you do.'

She gazed up at him, and a magical haze enveloped her as his previous tentative smile was replaced with a full-blown one, lighting up everything from his sparkling eyes to the curve of his lips.

'They're finished. Anyone for chips?' Nick's jovial comment brought Lila back to earth.

'Sure. Why not. I shouldn't be starving after that gigantic hunk of Christmas cake, but I am. But doesn't your mom have dinner planned?'

'Not a proper meal. It'll only be sandwiches and stuff. She knows we always visit the fish and chip van, doesn't she, mate?' Nick poked Grant's arm, and Lila's heart sunk as he turned to face them. With the joy gone from his face and his shoulders drooping, he'd aged ten years in the last few seconds.

'You both do what you like. I'm heading on back.'

Before either of them could stop him, Grant strode off through the crowd.

'What was all that about?' Lila asked.

'I'm an idiot,' Nick groused. 'This carol singing was Belle's favourite part of Christmas, and once she and Grant got together they'd always buy their chips afterwards and sneak off out on

38

the quay alone. I've heard them say it was their special time in the middle of the holiday chaos.' He rubbed at his eyes, blinking back tears. 'We'd better get after him.'

She grabbed his arm. 'Leave him alone for now. He'll be all right later.' Lila discreetly crossed her fingers. 'If the offer's still open, you can treat me to some of the famous chips.'

'You're on.' Nick laced his arm around her waist. 'All the better to stop you getting knocked over in all this lot. More than a few people have spent the afternoon in the Red Lion and probably popped in for another round during the singing. They're distinctly on the merry side by now.'

Lila didn't protest and let herself be steered over to the mobile chip van parked near the harbour wall. The crowds were thinning out now as people either headed home or went to carry on the festivities elsewhere.

'Salt and vinegar?' Nick asked.

'Is there any other way to eat them?'

She struggled to appear cheerful, but her mind couldn't erase the snapshot of Grant's defeated expression.

They took their chips and walked all the way along the outer quay. Faint sounds of laughter and people talking drifted across the water and mixed with the sound of gentle waves slapping up against the wall.

'I don't think he'll ever move on from Belle. It finished him.' Nick's comment came across almost as a warning, and Lila wasn't sure how to respond. 'Would you like to go into Truro with me tomorrow? There's a Christmas market going on and it'll be packed, but I think you'd enjoy it.'

'But surely you don't want to battle the traffic and crowds of people?'

His bright blue eyes, the replicas of Belle's, shone as they rested on her. 'With your company it'd be an adventure.'

'Can I let you know in the morning?' Lila tiptoed around his offer, not wanting to be too blunt. 'Let's walk on back. I don't know about you, but I could do with a cup of tea.'

'That sounded very English,' he laughed.

Lila would bet everything she owned that Grant was hiding out in the guest cottage. She didn't intend to go to bed tonight without talking to him, whether he liked it or not.

5

Grant startled at the knock on his door. He should've guessed Lila wouldn't let it be. 'Come in. It's unlocked.'

'I could be one of the famous Cornish smugglers or an axe-murderer for all you know,' Lila reprimanded as she sauntered in. 'You made Nick feel terrible. I stopped him running after you, but you should go and see him right now to apologise.'

He leapt from the sofa and planted himself in front of her. 'What right have you got to tell me what to do?' A flash of embarrassment lit up her face and he took a step backwards. 'Sorry. I don't know what came over me. I shouldn't have yelled.'

'Doesn't being angry all the time gnaw at you?' Lila murmured.

'Do you blame me?'

'Yes, and no.'

He scoffed. 'That's real clear.'

Lila glanced over his shoulder. 'Oh, you've got a kitchen. Make me a cup of tea.'

'Do you always boss people around?'

'Only if I care about them and they need it.' Lila's eyes widened. 'Oh, now it's my turn to be sorry.'

He didn't answer, and hurried away with his heart thumping. 'Milk and sugar.'

'Yes, please. Can I help?'

'No. Stay there.' Grant jerked back around. 'Sorry. I'm being rude again. Why do you bring out the worst in me? I usually have a vestige of good manners.'

'I'm pleased to hear it.' Her dry response forced him to smile. 'See, you don't need to glower all the time.'

It's safer. He'd put a wall between himself and the world after losing Belle and got used to the narrow confines of his new life. 'Why don't you sit down, and I'll see to the tea.'

'Sounds good. I can manage that.'

She shrugged off her black coat, tossing it on the back of the sofa.

Grant made the tea, gathered up two mugs and fetched the carton of milk from the fridge. He sneaked a glance over his shoulder at Lila stretched out in one of the large armchairs by the fire with her stocking feet resting on the coffee table. Her black leather boots lay abandoned on the carpet, and something about her obvious ease rattled him. Grant sloshed too much milk into his mug, forcing him to dump half of it away in the sink.

'There's the sugar. Help yourself.' He set a brimming mug of tea and a spoon down in front of her. 'I've got a tin of Edith's homemade gingerbreads if you're hungry.'

'No, thanks. I'm still full of chips.' Lila gave him a shrewd stare. 'Nick never meant to hurt you.'

'I know.' Grant lowered himself into the chair opposite her and drank some tea before speaking again. 'I over-reacted. It's a fault of mine these days.'

He sighed. 'If I'm completely honest, Nick stirred up a good memory.'

'But I'm guessin' it swooped in out of the blue and took you by surprise.'

He nodded. 'That's the way of it, and some days I handle it better than others.' Grant struggled to be polite. 'Were the chips good?'

Lila beamed. 'Awesome. Makes me never want to eat another skinny french fry again as long as I live.'

'Quite right too.'

She sipped her tea and gave him another thoughtful stare over the top of her mug. 'Maybe another day we'll eat some together.'

'Maybe.'

A secretive smile brightened her eyes, bringing out the flecks of gold he'd noticed when they first met. Lila set down her empty mug and reached to pick up one of her boots. 'We ought to go and join everyone else. Edith's got supper ready.' She tugged it on over her dark skinny jeans and repeated the procedure with the other one. 'Haven't you seen a woman put on a pair of boots before?'

Grant flushed.

'It's all right. I'll let you off this time.' Lila stood and picked up her coat to slip it back on. 'Come on, cowboy.'

Making any sort of protest would be fruitless, so he didn't even make an attempt.

Grant's mercurial mood changes threw her for a loop. After his outburst in the cottage, he'd slipped back to his charming, friendly self as if nothing happened. He apologised to Nick and won Edith around by eating a mound of sandwiches, and enough of the hand-held mince pies to sink the proverbial battleship.

English mince pies were Lila's new favourite thing. When Edith first offered her one, she'd been puzzled. Only the day before, they'd been talking about cooking, and Lila discovered that what she called ground beef the English called mince. She'd put two and two together and been confused to be offered a tiny meat pie with powdered sugar on top. After she ventured to ask the question, and the laughter finally died down, Grant explained that the filling consisted of dried fruit, suet, nuts, spices and usually some sort of alcohol. She mentally connected it then to the similar thing they had in the States, but there the filling was far softer and used to make a thick regular-sized pie.

'It's not powdered sugar either, it's icing sugar.'

'Is that my British English lesson for the day?' she retorted.

'You'll have homework to do tonight, young lady, if you answer the teacher back again.' Grant's quip startled her, and everyone else, judging by the surprised glances going around the room. Grant cracking a joke was obviously on a par with the likelihood of Santa Claus coming down the chimney tomorrow night — something they'd all like to believe could happen but more realistically doubted.

Nick yawned. 'I'm going to bed.' He glanced at Lila. 'Let me know in the morning what you decide about Truro.'

Pretty sure that Edith was watching her reaction Lila made do with simply thanking him and reached for another mince pie.

'I'll help you clear up, love.' John assured his wife, but Grant sprang to his feet.

'No, you won't. You two have done enough. Lila and I will get this. You have an early night.'

We will? 'That's a great idea. We'd be happy to.' She didn't miss Nick's sharp glance as he left the room.

'Are you sure?' Edith asked. 'I must admit it's been a long day, and all the family will be here for tea tomorrow, so I've more baking to do in the morning.'

'You must let me help then,' Lila offered. 'I'm not gonna take no for an answer.'

'But I thought you're going into Truro with Nick.'

She shook her head. 'He offered, but

48

I hadn't made up my mind. I'm not much for Christmas shopping crowds.' Not strictly true, but a good way out of the dilemma. 'I'd prefer to learn how to make mince pies.'

'It'll be nice to have your company. Belle used to . . . ' Edith struggled to compose herself. 'We always made mince pies together on Christmas Eve.'

'And drank sherry at the same time.' John teased. 'They chugged back more than they put in the pies.'

'Stop your complaining and take me to bed.' Edith poked her husband's ribs. 'If you two aren't sure where the dishes go, just leave them out and I'll put them away in the morning.'

'Off you go.' Grant shooed her away.

Left on their own, Lila hesitated, unsure what to say or do next.

'Do you prefer to wash or wipe?'

She stared, uncomprehending.

'The dishes?'

'I don't care. Wipe, I guess.'

'Unusual woman,' he observed with a wry smile. 'They usually prefer to wash.

I think it's a control thing to make sure it's done properly.'

Lila held her tongue. She'd almost joked that Belle was the worst when it came to doing the dishes in the flat they'd shared but didn't want to upset him.

'She was a bit of a slob, wasn't she? Housework and Belle didn't mix well. If I hadn't taken on doing most of the cleaning, we'd have lived in a pigsty.' Grant's affection rang out loud and clear.

Lila blinked back tears. He took a step closer and reached for her hands, encompassing them with his own. As the warmth from his fingers penetrated through her skin, Lila's cheeks flamed.

'Hey, it's good to talk about her again. I've avoided it far too long.'

'The dishes,' she mumbled, and Grant let go one of her hands to touch her chin, encouraging her to glance up at him. Lila's heart pounded as a slow, teasing smile spread over his face.

'I forgot the book I wanted . . . ' Nick

burst back into the room and came to a grinding halt. 'Sorry. I didn't mean to interrupt anything.'

'You weren't.' Grant dropped his hands away. 'We were debating who'd wash and who'd wipe.'

'Oh, yeah, that's exactly what it looked like.' Nick's sarcasm made Lila wince. Putting a wedge between the two men wasn't on her agenda. 'I'll leave you to it.' He fixed his attention on her. 'I assume you won't be accompanying me to Truro in the morning?'

'Well, no, I've promised your mother I'd help her with some baking.'

'Really. I'll see you both tomorrow.' He stalked out without another word.

'I'm sorry,' Lily murmured.

'What for? You didn't do anything wrong.' Grant shrugged. 'Neither did I, come to think of it. I didn't plan to kiss you . . . Well, I don't mean I didn't want to.'

His endearing awkwardness was touching.

'What I meant to say, or rather ask, is

if I had kissed you, would I have been treading on anyone else's toes?' Now his burning cheeks matched her own. 'I don't mean to assume you'd have wanted it either, but . . .'

Lila pressed a finger to his lips. 'No toe-treading. I promise. That's all I'm saying for now. Let's do the dishes.'

'Dishes. Right.' For one wonderful moment, they held each other's gaze before breaking away, almost by mutual consent.

The undeniable attraction between herself and Grant stirred up endless possible complications. If she had any sense, she'd get the next train out of Cornwall. But as her mother always said, common sense never was Lila's forte. She'd take her chances and see what Christmas Eve brought.

6

Grant dressed in his running clothes and quietly made his way out towards the front gate. Over the last three years, he'd used running as a way to push away his grief, but today he simply buzzed with a rush of excess energy. He did a few stretches up against the wall to loosen his hamstrings and started off down the road, empty of both people and cars this early in the day.

He headed up towards the cliffs and picked up his pace as he settled into a steady rhythm. Later he must put things straight with Nick. He wouldn't lie to his old friend the way he did last night. What exactly Nick *had* interrupted he couldn't be sure, but in another couple of seconds he might've found out. Grant wasn't certain he could have resisted the temptation to kiss Lila, so maybe he should thank

Nick for saving him from himself.

Grant breathed in the fresh, salty air and sped up to put more distance between him and Mendelby House. Rain or shine, he always took this same familiar route, the three miles over to the next small village of St. Aubyn and back again. Apart from his minor meltdown over the chips last night, his experience coming back to Port Carne was overwhelmingly positive. Returning to this place, which he'd grown to love, and sorely missed, was doing wonders for him. For the first time in years he'd slept heavily and woken refreshed.

As he reached the top of the hill leading down into St. Aubyn, he turned around and began the long run back. Lila drifted into his mind and he couldn't help smiling. He'd met other more traditionally beautiful women since losing Belle, but none came close to interesting him the way she did. Something about her intriguing southern drawl, teasing smile and sharp wit wouldn't leave him alone. Grant wasn't sure how to handle the possibility that the rest of his life might not have to be an emotional wasteland. He'd loved once. Completely and utterly. The idea of risking his heart a second time frightened him. *Slow down. Take a deep breath.* He took himself literally and reduced his pace to a slow jog. Instead of pondering things it was too soon to consider, he thought about what to do with the rest of the day. He coasted along Seaview Terrace and back to Mendelby House.

He needed to go somewhere and buy a Christmas present for Lila, because he'd brought gifts for the rest of the family with him. Grant's limited experience of women and gifts was enough to know they could be a minefield. Something too personal wouldn't work, but the reverse could also be true.

He walked the last few metres and started to do his stretches again to cool down.

'So this is how you stay so fit.' Lila's laughter from somewhere behind him startled him into almost toppling over, but he managed to right himself. He caught Lila checking him out, the gold flecks in her eyes brighter than ever.

'Edith's busy cooking breakfast, and she obviously thinks we're going to put in a twelve-hour day down the local tin mine by the amount of food she's fixing.'

'I'm all right because I've done my six miles. I can afford to stuff myself now. You, on the other hand . . . ' Grant teased.

'It's not polite to comment on a lady's figure unless you're being complimentary.'

'And what makes you think I wasn't going to be?'

Lila folded her arms and fake-glared at him. 'I can't imagine.'

She looked pretty much perfect to him. Grant's mouth curved into a smile, and a tinge of pink coloured her cheeks as she clearly read his thoughts.

'I'd better go and take a shower.' He made no effort to move and neither did she. 'Aren't you afraid you'll be mistaken for Christmas tree and someone will stick a star on your head?'

Grant pointed to her thigh-length red jumper decorated with a garish fir tree, complete with gold baubles and strands of tinsel that fluttered in the breeze.

'You're out of touch where fashion is concerned,' Lila retorted. 'Ugly Christmas sweaters are all the rage again. People even have ugly sweater parties and competitions.'

'I should think yours would win hands down.'

'Huh!'

The idea baffled him, but sometimes giving up was the wisest move around women. 'Anyway, that's enough hassling you for a while. I'm starved.'

'Fair enough. I'll get my revenge you know.'

You already have simply by standing there and rekindling an attraction I shouldn't be feeling. Grant walked away while he had the willpower to resist.

Lila allowed the crisp morning air to

bathe her face and calm the tell-tale blush that'd give her away if she walked back inside now. She'd never been attracted to conventionally handsome men, but Grant's new leaner, more angular look appealed to her — too much if she was being honest. Slowly she made her way up the path.

Nick appeared in the doorway. 'We're ready to eat. Mum wants us all there together. We always used to do this on Christmas Eve and then all go our own separate ways until tea-time.' He frowned. 'The tradition kind of fell by the wayside after we lost Belle.'

Lila touched his arm. 'I get it. Let's go.'

'I hope you're hungry, because Mum won't let us leave the kitchen until it's all eaten.' Nick chuckled.

I can afford to stuff myself now. You on the other hand . . . Remembering Grant's wry amusement sent a warm tingling sensation coursing through Lila. 'I'm ready. Lead the way.'

Edith appeared in the small hall and

ushered her into the kitchen. 'Lila love, come in and help yourself. Grant will be back to join us in a minute or so. The boy would go out for a run this morning, even though he's skinny as a whippet these days and doesn't need to lose another ounce.' She patted her round stomach and smiled. 'Unlike some of us.'

Without needing to be asked twice, Lila picked up a plate and started to load it from the multitude of dishes set out on the kitchen counter. Skipping lunch might be a wise move, considering there'd be a big family tea this afternoon that she'd been warned would consist of a huge amount of food, not merely a cup of tea and a cookie. There would also be a late supper before they went to church tonight. All of that didn't take into consideration tomorrow's Christmas dinner. Lila's jeans tightened thinking about it all.

'Any left for me?' Grant said as he sauntered in, and Lila didn't trust herself to answer. She wished she wasn't so aware of his clean scent and the way his hair clung in dark curls to the back of his neck. 'You've even got my favourite black pudding. You're a star.'

She sneaked a glance at the dark slices of dried-up meat he shovelled onto his plate.

'This boy spent too long living up north. No one in Cornwall eats the stuff.' Edith sighed, but added a happy smile.

'What is it?' Lila's curiosity got the better of her.

'Blood sausage. It's delicious. Try a piece.' He speared one and popped it onto her plate before she could stop him. 'Down here they prefer hog's pudding. Tasteless stuff.' Nick instantly protested, and they launched into a friendly argument about the varying merits of the different kinds of sausage.

'Try this. It's much better.' Nick deposited a lighter-coloured sausage patty in front of her. 'Give us your opinion.'

She threw Edith a helpless glance but only got a shrug in response. Making sure to cut similarly sized bites, she tried each in turn, chewed carefully and thought before she answered. Her mother always said if you can't say something nice don't say anything at all, but that wouldn't work in this case. 'They're both fine, but to be honest I prefer our Tennessee country sausage. It's got a spicy kick to it.'

John Warren gave her a thumbs-up sign behind the two younger men's backs.

'The woman's got no taste,' Grant declared, and Nick vehemently agreed. Exactly what she'd hoped for.

Edith pulled rank and made it clear who was in charge. 'Right, that's enough of your nonsense. Get on and eat before it gets cold.'

Lily returned to wading through the delicious pile of bacon, eggs, tomatoes and mushrooms, plus something she'd been told was fried bread. The crispy golden triangles were exactly what their name suggested. For someone coming from the south, where they were great believers in frying everything they could lay their hands on, this was a new and dangerous discovery.

'Are you still going into Truro today? Only, I could do with a lift,' Grant asked Nick. 'I've got some Christmas shopping to do.'

Lila hoped Nick wouldn't ignore his old friend's olive branch, because she didn't want them at odds with each other, especially not over her.

'I suppose I could.' Nick's grudging reply wasn't over-enthusiastic, but at least he hadn't refused outright. 'Let's get cracking before the crowds get unreal.' He pushed away his empty plate and stood up. 'Anything you need while we're out, Mum?'

'I don't think so, love.' Edith's indulgent gaze rested on her son. 'Make sure you're back by four o'clock.' She wagged her finger at them both. 'Don't spend too long in the Miner's Arms either. I know you pair of old.' Turning her attention to her husband, she fixed him with a stern glare. 'And don't you suggest joining them. When you close up at lunchtime, I've got a long list of jobs for you to do here.'

Lila's throat tightened. Her parents behaved in exactly the same way, and she longed to experience that level of loving, good-natured bickering with her own husband one day. She startled as Grant touched her shoulder.

'Good luck with your mince pie lesson. I'll look forward to tasting the results.' He tugged gently on one of the strands of tinsel decorating her jumper. 'Be careful you don't get tangled up in the rolling pin.'

'I'll try not to. Happy shopping.'

His bright green eyes sparkled. 'It's bound to be great. Christmas Eve. All the last-minute shoppers. Any man's idea of — '

'Don't say it,' Lila stopped him, guessing Edith wouldn't care to hear his blunt assessment of the joys of Christmas shopping. 'Next year plan ahead.'

'Oh, I will do, don't worry.' He held her gaze before turning away, and Lila sagged back into the chair. This should give her a reprieve for several hours before he returned to continue whatever they'd unwittingly started.

7

It'd taken an excruciating two hours, twenty-four minutes and ten seconds, not that he'd counted, to track down a suitable present for Lila, and the pint of Doom Bar in front of him was Grant's reward. He sank half of the refreshing bitter ale in one swallow and set the glass back down with a contented sigh.

'Better?' Nick cracked a smile, the first of the morning.

'I will be when I finish this and get another.' Grant drained the rest of his pint. 'My round.' He picked up their glasses and headed back to the bar, quickly catching the barmaid's eye. He'd better get his apology to Nick over with or they'd be back in Port Carne still half-avoiding each other. 'There you go. Get that down.' He sat back down. 'I didn't tell you the complete truth last night, mate.'

'I know that. I'm not dumb.'

Grant shifted in the seat. He'd inherited his taciturn father's dislike of talking about his feelings. After his wife's sudden death, Ian Hawkins got rid of every trace of her from their home and never spoke about her again. To a bewildered eight-year-old, it'd been a brutal shock he'd never got over. He'd frustrated Belle on more than one occasion with his inability to open up, something he bitterly regretted now. Grant took a couple of deep, steadying breaths.

'I don't need you to spill your guts. Just be honest.'

Easier said than done. Grant tentatively explained what'd almost happened with Lila and the fact he didn't have a clue what he felt for her.

'See. Didn't kill you, did it?' Nick probed. 'Maybe I'm more in touch with my feminine side,' he joked. 'I picked up on something between the two of you the minute you met.'

Grant idly rubbed his unshaven jaw.

66

'Doesn't it bother you?'

Nick's eyes narrowed. 'Why? Because I find Lila attractive too, or because you were married to my sister?'

'Either. Both.'

'Hey, we've fancied the same girls before now and we're still friends.' Nick toyed with his glass. 'As to Belle, I don't expect you to spend the rest of your life alone. That'd suck and she wouldn't want it.'

'But how can you know that?' Grant blurted out. 'I've never understood why people trot out that old chestnut.'

'I won't ask what if it'd been the other way around, because you know the answer deep down.' Nick took a long draw at his beer and wiped the foam from his mouth. 'Would it help you to know she told me so?'

'What the devil are you on about?'

Nick sighed. 'The night before you got married, we had a few drinks and she got a bit emotional. Belle told me how much she loved you, and that if anything ever happened to her she couldn't bear the thought of you being lonely.' He attempted to smile. 'Mind you, she also said if the woman wasn't good enough, she'd come back and haunt you.'

'You're making this up to make me feel better.'

'Why would I do that? If I lay more of a guilt trip on you, it ups my chances with Lila. I'm not a saint.'

Nick's words made sense, but Grant still couldn't get his head around it all. 'But why did she do it, Nick? Why go swimming in frigid water when she'd been having heart problems?' He leaned forward, resting his elbows on the table. 'If I'd known before the swim, I could've stopped her. I always tried to protect her. Keep her safe. Why didn't she tell me she wasn't well and let me help? I would never have gone back to London if I'd known.' It'd about finished Grant to discover at the inquest that Belle scheduled a doctor's appointment on the day after her death to discuss some heart rhythm problems and light-headedness she'd been experiencing. It'd struck at the very core of what he'd believed about the strength of their love.

'Because Belle always lived life to the fullest. You know that. It's one reason you fell for her in the first place. No restrictions. No holding back. She didn't know any other way. She'd done the Boxing Day Polar Bear Plunge since she was fifteen. Nothing and no one could stop my dumb sister.' Nick's voice cracked.

Tears pulled at Grant's throat, shutting it down. Even if every word Nick said was the absolute truth, that didn't make it any easier for him to live with.

'Cheerful pair, aren't we?' Nick teased. 'We'd better get back to Port Carne to prepare for the family onslaught. Thank heavens they'll leave again by early evening. Three hours is as much as I can take.'

Not sure I'll be able to take three minutes.

'Lila will be there. You'll hack it.' Nick's smile disappeared. 'Don't make

Belle your excuse for not giving things a try with her.'

A trickle of hope sneaked into Grant's bloodstream, and he wondered if this New Year might actually be one to look forward to. Even if things didn't work out with Lila, he'd no intention of letting himself slide backwards again.

★   ★   ★

'That's the lot. We're done.' Edith wiped her floury hands on her apron and beamed at Lila. 'You've been a big help, my 'andsome.'

'I've enjoyed every minute.' It'd never been her aim to replace Belle, but hopefully her company made today's baking efforts go more smoothly. They'd laughed, reminisced, drunk too much of the notorious sherry, and wiped away more than a few tears. Now the aroma of dozens of fresh mince pies, sausage rolls and scones infused the kitchen. That was on top of the cocktail pasties, chocolate Yule log and saffron cake Lila collected after lunch from the local bakery. While they were baking, she'd copied out several recipes to try back home in Nashville, although buying a bottle of sherry wouldn't be on her list of new things to try. The strong, sweet drink wasn't to her taste, although she'd indulged in a couple of glasses to keep Edith company.

She smiled, thinking about the present she'd found for Grant while out on her bakery expedition. Lila had poked around a couple of the charity shops and picked up a cool Victorian nightgown before spotting something that should make Grant laugh tomorrow. On the rare occasions when he'd let go and showed his joy, it'd made her knees weaken and her heart race.

'I'm going up to put on a clean jumper and skirt and comb my hair,' Edith announced as she finished putting away the dishes Lila had wiped. 'Stick the kettle on to boil and we'll have a quick cup when I come back down.'

The need to have tea an hour before her family arrived for a meal actually called tea bewildered Lila but she didn't argue. Left on her own, she followed Edith's orders before stepping out onto the back patio. She shivered as a sharp easterly wind blew in off the sea, cutting through the weak sunshine struggling hard to brighten a dull, cloudy day.

'No weird woolly Christmas tree to keep you warm?' Grant's deep voice startled her and he slipped an arm around her shoulder.

For a second she didn't get his joke, but suddenly remembered the sweater he'd mocked earlier in the day. Before helping Edith, she'd changed into a thin long-sleeved green T-shirt to stop herself from overheating in the tiny kitchen.

'You'll need to put it back on for church tonight. Think solid granite walls and very little in the way of central heating. My secret weapon is thermal underwear.'

'Sounds enticing. I hope they never employ you to be their PR man,' Lila teased. Instead of being sensible and moving away from Grant, she snuggled a little closer.

'It's not very likely.'

'I guess not. Your students would miss you.'

He frowned. 'I forgot you don't know.'

'Know what?'

'I changed jobs.'

Lila sensed a touch of awkwardness about his reply and wondered if she should change the subject.

'Don't worry. I'm not going to fall apart talking about it.' Grant's wry smile eased her concern. 'I couldn't handle teaching after I lost Belle.' He shook his head. 'Couldn't handle much, to be honest.'

She wondered if he'd ever confessed this much to anyone else.

'I resigned and didn't do much for a while except live on my savings and feel sorry for myself.'

'You had every right to — '

'Grieve, yes,' he interrupted, 'but not give up completely. Belle would've smacked me from here to Land's End. Eventually I picked up a few odd jobs for the money and to fill the time. I'd done a lot of carpentry with my father years ago, and it all came back to me when I got a saw in my hands again.' He shrugged. 'New-agers might call it therapy. Practical men prefer the words hard work.' He cracked a smile. 'I started my own small business about a year ago. It'll never make me a fortune, but I don't need one.'

'Wow, that's cool. What kind of stuff do you make?'

'I can turn my hand to most things, but a lot of kitchen cabinets, small tables and the occasional chair. People are starting to appreciate artisan crafts again.'

Lila eased out of his arms and took hold of his hands, cradling them with her own and rubbing her fingers over his tanned work-roughened skin. 'They're capable hands. I admire people who can create useful things.' She glanced up to catch him blushing under her scrutiny and instantly let go. 'Sorry. I didn't mean to embarrass you.'

'I don't embarrass *that* easily,' he murmured.

'Good.' Lila trembled, as nervous as she'd been at sixteen when Walt Manning kissed her in the back seat of the Franklin Cinema.

'It must be tea time.'

'Tea time?' she croaked.

'I believe I need to do a mince pie check. Mark you out of ten on your baking abilities,' Grant declared, and gave her a mischievous wink.

Later would be time enough to worry. For now she'd embrace the spirit of Christmas and goodwill to all men — especially Grant Hawkins.

8

Grant wedged himself into a rickety folding chair in the corner of the room and hoped he'd be overlooked. The crowd of assorted aunts, uncles, cousins, nieces and nephews were all managing to talk and eat at the same time. It'd been tolerable when he'd come here with Belle, because she'd embraced everything about the holidays and nobody had appeared to notice his silence.

'I take it the Hawkins mob aren't like this?' Lila whispered, perching on a piano stool next to him.

'Hardly.' This wasn't the place for a discussion of his family, or lack of one. 'How about yours?' He'd kill two birds with one stone to find out more about her and deflect attention from himself at the same time.

'Oh, yeah, we could give them a run for their money.' A wide grin lit up her lovely face. 'No one in the Caswell family comes under the heading of shy and retiring. We usually get together at my uncle's farm outside of Memphis because he's got the biggest house. Everyone comes for at least a couple of days, and I spend the time eating far too much, talking nonstop, brokering fights between the children, and battling to get into one of the two bathrooms.' Her eyes narrowed. 'Sounds appalling to you, doesn't it?'

He obviously hadn't covered up his horror well enough. There must be something about being a solitary, quiet child that drew him to exuberant sociable women. Grant suspected there might be a psychological study in there somewhere.

'Would you believe I'd expected a quiet Christmas here?' Lila's rueful smile made him laugh.

'Seriously?'

'Yeah. Remember, I didn't know about all these people.' She gestured around the room.

'Or about me.' A tinge of colour warmed her cheeks, pleasing him unduly.

'I certainly didn't expect you.' Lila's earnest tone pulled him up sharply. Something non-flirtatious and serious lurked behind her words, and he ached to find out what she meant.

Edith clapped her hands. 'Listen up, everyone. If you haven't met young Lila yet, make sure you say hallo.' She pointed in their direction, and Grant considered pulling a Harry Potter and disappearing into thin air. 'She and Belle were good friends, and she's from Nashville, Tennessee. Lila helped me in the kitchen this morning and the mince pies are all her work.' Her gaze rested on Grant next. 'I know *everyone* remembers Grant. He hasn't been in a while, but we're some pleased he's spending Christmas with us.'

He managed to nod and half-smile at everyone now staring blatantly at him.

'Prepare to face your doom.' Lila's soft laughter eased the knots in his stomach and he made an effort to return her smile. 'How about a quiet walk when they've all gone?'

He nodded, not trusting himself to speak.

'That's a date.' She wagged her finger at him. 'Don't grimace. I didn't mean it *that* way.' Lila jumped up to shake hands with Edith's brother, and the elusive moment disappeared.

★   ★   ★

The front door closed as the last Warren cousin left, and Lila silently exhaled her relief. It'd been a challenge to cope with all the conversations and questions about her relationship with Belle. The overwhelming urge to lie down somewhere quiet and alone swept through her, and she could only imagine how Grant felt. She'd sneaked an occasional glance in his direction and picked up on the tight line of his jaw and the struggle in his stern, dark eyes. All she remembered Belle telling her about Grant's family was that his mother had died when he was very young.

'Can I help to clear up?' she offered, but almost before the words left her mouth Grant grabbed her arm and flashed Edith one of his winning smiles.

'I'll bet anything you and John could do with some time to yourselves. I know Nick's heading off down to the Red Lion to play in the darts tournament, so I thought I'd take this lady out for a breath of fresh air.'

'You'll find plenty of that, all right.' John's dry tone made his wife laugh. 'The wind's cutting in around some-thing fierce tonight. The forecast's not good either.'

'Go on with you.' Edith shooed at them both. 'Church starts at eleven. We'll see you there if you don't come back home first.'

Lila opened her mouth to assure Edith they wouldn't be gone long but caught Grant's warning glance and shut up. A tingle of pleasure zipped through her at the idea of him wanting her company for the rest of the evening.

'I'm going to put on something warmer and grab a coat,' he said, and strode off towards the back door, leaving her to face Edith's inquisitive stare.

'I'd better do the same.' Lila raced towards the stairs as if she was being chased, only slowing down when she reached the sanctuary of her bedroom. She put on the Christmas jumper and the same warm boots and coat she'd worn for last night's carol singing. With her wool hat and gloves tucked into the pockets for later, she should survive anything an icy church could throw at her. Before she left, she put on her oversized Christmas-tree earrings and added a necklace made up of flashing mini-Christmas lights. If nothing else, it'd make Grant smile. She sauntered back downstairs and found him waiting for her.

'You certainly believe in getting into the festive spirit.' Grant's rich laughter filled the hall.

'And you have a problem with that?'

'No.' He shrugged. 'I'm coming to understand better now why you and Belle became friends.' He stared down at his feet. 'Maybe I'm envious.'

The unexpected comment took her breath away.

'Are you ready for our walk?'

'That's it? You're leaving the conversation there?'

His dark expression pleaded with her to let up on him, but Lila knew if she did they'd never get anywhere. Belle had shared many of her frustrations long-distance, and her husband's taciturn nature frequently came out top of the list.

'We'll walk, but you'll talk at the same time,' she said.

'Or?'

She fixed him with a firm stare. 'Or I'll leave you to it and join Nick in the pub.'

'You wouldn't.'

'Try me.' Her heart thudded in her chest as she waited for his response.

'Fine. Let's go.'

She'd heard more gracious concession speeches but chose not to push him too far. At least not tonight. Lila linked her arm through his, called out to Edith that they were off, and steered him towards the front door before he could change his mind. 'Where are we going?' she asked.

'Along the cliff road towards St. Aubyn. It's too far to go all the way tonight, but . . . '

'It's your favourite.'

Grant nodded and grasped hold of her hand, tucking it into his pocket. 'Most people think the walk over to Pendruid in the other direction is prettier, but this is more rugged and changeable in its moods.'

'Like you,' Lila ventured, falling into step with him as they headed away from Seaview Terrace. Within minutes the only light came from the moon, the few stars visible through the clouds and Grant's bright torch.

'Belle often got mad at me,' he plunged right in, taking her by surprise.

'Why?' She knew one side of the story but needed his to complete the picture.

Grant sighed. 'I suppose you need to hear about my family first.'

'Only if you want to talk about them.'

'Want?' He scoffed. 'Want isn't the right word.'

'Need?'

'I suppose.' Grant shone the torch in front of them. 'Be careful where you're walking.'

She surveyed the narrow rocky path and wondered at his sanity. 'You run here? You must be crazy.' Tonight's rough waves battered against the cliff, reminding her how close they were to the edge and a plummeting drop to the sharp rocks beneath them.

'In daylight.' She couldn't miss his mischievous grin. 'I'm only half-mad.'

They didn't hurry, and as they walked Grant's reticence ebbed away and his story emerged. Lila bit back tears as he explained with no hint of emotion about his mother's death. Her heart broke for the shy eight-year-old boy, and she couldn't get her head around how Grant must've felt to be bluntly told the awful news by his inarticulate father.

'It's why I dragged my heels over starting a family with Belle. I don't know how to be a good father, and I won't subject any child to what I went through.'

The unutterably sad statement broke her heart, and she thought carefully before speaking again. 'Belle would've taught you. You'd have done it together. Both parents don't have to be noisy extroverts, and you'd give a child different things.' She suddenly recalled something he'd told her. 'Maybe your dad's way of communicating was through the carpentry he taught you. That must've taken patience and kindness.'

He gave her a shrewd stare. 'You're smart. I've never thought of it that way.'

'I'm guessing your father wouldn't want us to, but I feel sorry for him.'

'Not sure I'd go that far.'

'Did he love your mother?'

'Of course he did.'

Lila squeezed his hand. 'Think of it. Out of nowhere, he loses her and is left to raise you alone. He erases her existence and refuses to talk about her because he can't cope any other way.'

'I couldn't speak to anyone about Belle either.' Grant's voice cracked and he stopped walking. 'Oh, God, I'm no different from him.'

She slid her arms around his waist and rested her head against his warm chest. 'Yes, you are. What're we doing now?'

'Talking, I suppose.'

The grudging reply made her smile. She gently kissed his cheek. 'See. You can do this.'

'I really want to.'

'That's half the battle.'

'I could . . . '

A chilling scream echoed through the darkness, and Lila clutched onto Grant.

9

'You need to let go of me and I'll try to see what's going on,' Grant pleaded.

'Do you think someone's fallen off the cliff?'

If they had, Grant didn't give much for their chances.

'I doubt it. It's probably a gull. They're noisy devils.' Lila's eyebrows raised in disbelief. She didn't believe him any more than he believed himself.

'Don't you dare move from here.'

'I won't. I'm not stupid.'

'I know, but I'm a worrier.' He didn't need to spell it out because she understood him.

Grant forced himself to stand still and simply listen. Apart from the noisy gusting wind and the roar of the waves slamming against the rocks, he heard nothing out of place. He scanned the area around them with a wide sweep of his torch and cautiously started to move forward. 'Hallo,' he yelled. He reached the spot where an old, narrow flight of broken-down steps led to Porth Garen, a sheltered spot on the coastline too small to be termed a beach but popular with the locals. At one time there'd been a handrail, but it'd mostly broken off years ago and never been replaced. These days only the foolhardy took the chance on going down that way. He edged close to the top of the steps and braced himself against the harsh wind, struggling to keep his balance. 'Is anyone there?' *Idiot. You sound like a medium conducting a séance.*

'Help. For God's sake help me,' a thin, eerie voice wailed through the suffocating darkness, and Grant took a couple of steadying breaths.

'Stay where you are.' It'd be foolish of him to attempt to climb down alone. 'I'm going to fetch my friend to help too, and I'll be right back.' He had to trust the person could hear him. He suppressed the urge to run, and walked as fast as he dared back towards Lila.

'Oh, thank goodness.' She flung herself at him and her whole body trembled as he held on to her. 'I . . . don't do well in the dark.'

'You should've said.' Lila's unexpected touch of vulnerability took him by surprise.

'And what would you have done? Ignored the fact we thought we heard someone scream? Did you find anything?'

Grant ignored her first two questions and quickly explained the situation. 'I don't know if they're hurt or what's happened. I didn't want to go down there on my own.'

'I'm glad you've got some sense. Come on, let's see what we can do.'

The weakening light from Grant's torch flickered, and he prayed it'd hold out a while longer. 'When we get there, give your phone a try in case there's any signal.' He let go of Lila's hand and inched towards the cliff edge. 'We're back,' he yelled into the darkness.

'I can't hold on much longer.'

'He's panicking,' Lila said. 'We haven't got time to waste.'

'You think it's a man?'

'I'd guess a teenage boy.'

'Are you alone?' Grant shouted down.

'Yep. My friend made it all the way back up and left me here.'

Some friend.

'I . . . froze.' His voice rose in panic.

Lila touched Grant's arm. 'You'd better let me do this.'

'You? Are you crazy?' He caught a hint of her smile in the silvery moonlight.

'Is this the right time to let on that one of my hobbies is bouldering?' Lila tossed out. 'We've got steps here, so it shouldn't be a problem.'

'What the devil is bouldering?'

'Rock climbing without the use of ropes and harnesses.' She held back the fact she normally wore special shoes, used chalk to keep her hands dry, and did it with other people to spot her and place large soft mats for her to fall down on if needed. 'I've been doing it for ages.'

'But you design make-up shop window displays.'

She couldn't blame Grant for struggling to get his head around the idea, because her poor mother felt the same way. 'I love the adrenaline rush. I do a lot of off-piste skiing and paragliding too.'

'More to add to the list of things to talk about. You'd get your adrenaline fix tonight, that's for certain. Toss in the fact you'd be doing it in the dark, which you hate. And there's at least a force four gale blowing. Oh, I almost forgot, it's starting to drizzle.'

She ignored the hint of sarcasm. 'You're bigger than I am. It'd be harder for you and far less safe.'

Grant's white face stared back at her. If she came to any harm, he'd never forgive himself. 'Let me try my phone.' He waved it around, searching fruitlessly for a signal while she fought to dampen down her impatience. 'Damn,' Grant cursed and shoved it back in his pocket.

'We don't have any choice. By the time we fetch help from Port Carne, it'll be too late. He'll lose his grip and fall.' She bent down to tug off her boots and socks.

'What on earth are you doing?'

'Without my climbing shoes, it'll be safer to go barefoot.'

He grasped her arm. 'I can't let you do this. I'm going down.'

Lila pulled out of his tight grip. 'Now you're the one being an idiot. You know everything I'm saying makes sense, but your male ego won't give in.'

'It's nothing to do with that,' Grant yelled. 'I lost one woman I love, and I can't . . . ' His voice hitched on a sob.

She reached up to caress his cold, damp cheek. 'This is my choice to make.'

'Okay. I get it.' He threw up his hands. 'What can I do to help?'

Pray. 'Talk to the boy. Reassure him.'

'Father Christmas will put lots of

good things in your stocking after this.'

Lila appreciated his feeble attempt at a joke. 'I should hope so.' She plastered on a wide smile. 'Let's do this. Shine the light down to help me.'

'It's nearly gone.' A thread of fear inched through his words.

'Your phone. It'll give us more light. It doesn't need a signal for that.' While he fumbled with the phone, she quickly got rid of her hat and gloves, stowed them in her coat pocket, and added the earrings and necklace so they wouldn't get in her way. She tossed her coat down on the damp grass.

'The rain's easing off a bit,' he said.

The steps would already be treacherous, but Lila appreciated his effort to ease her misgivings. She turned around, groped to find handholds on either side of the steps, and reached down with her right foot.

'Hey, what's your name?' Grant's disembodied voice floated in and out of her awareness. 'Paul? Do you live in the village, Paul?'

Lila forcibly relaxed her muscles and kept going. The boy's replies got louder, giving her hope it wouldn't be much further before she reached him.

'I can see you!' came a shout.

She glanced down and could make out the vague shape of a face. Lila was pathetically grateful for the faint slivers of moonlight piercing the encompassing darkness. She blamed her fear on her eldest brother, who'd removed her bedside light bulb in the middle of a storm one night for fun and revelled in her hysterical reaction. 'Paul, how're you doing?'

'Better. But I'm tired, and . . . '

'I expect you're scared. I know I am,' Lila admitted. 'I'm gonna shift off the steps and hold on to the cliff while you clamber up past me. Then I'll be behind you all the way.'

'I can't do that!'

You've got to, or we're both toast. 'Yes, you can. You climbed down the steps. It's simply doing it in reverse.'

'But they're wet now and it's dark.'

Panic coursed through his voice. 'I should never have listened to my mate. Kenwyn Trevear's an idiot.'

Really? You think? 'Don't worry about him now.' Lila found the initial foot and handholds she needed. She blotted out the fear and trusted to her experience and instinct. Leaving the safety of the narrow steps, she clung to the granite cliff, and after a few steadying breaths she risked speaking again. 'Paul, go up the first step very slowly.' She heard the scrape of the boy's shoes on the rock and spotted his hand not far from her own. 'Good boy.' It took him two more steps to get clear of her. 'I'm coming over behind you now.' She made the move and stared up at Paul's jean-clad legs. One false move on his part and there'd be nothing she could do to save either of them. 'Keep going.'

'I can see your head, Paul,' Grant shouted, and Lila calculated they had another five steps to go before they'd be safe. *Four. Three. Two.* A stream of gravel rained down on her head, and Paul screamed. 'Dig your hands in,' she ordered and grabbed hold of his ankles, forcing her bare toes into jagged gaps in the step. Sharp pain stabbed through her feet and legs as she struggled to keep them both from falling. 'Are you steady now?' She gasped for breath.

'I think so.'

'Are you both all right?' Grant's deep voice trembled, and she ached to see his face again. She didn't know how, or if, she could be a lasting part of his life, but it wouldn't be for lack of trying on her part.

'Yeah, we're good,' Lila called back. 'You should be able to reach Paul's hands in a minute and help him up over the last bit.'

'Will do.'

Paul's last scramble for purchase sent more rocks cascading on her head, but she gritted her teeth and kept going.

'I've got him.' Grant's exhortation gave her a spurt of energy and she managed the last couple of steps. She spotted his large hands reaching for her through the darkness and used the last vestige of strength remaining in her legs to push herself up into his grasp. He hauled her over the cliff edge and sunk to his knees, wrapping his arms around her in a tight embrace. Lila's tears flowed freely and mixed with the rain. 'I thought you were . . . don't ever do that to me again.' Grant gulped for breath. 'We need to get Paul home.'

'I don't know if I can walk far.' Lila winced and stretched out her legs.

Grant swept the glowing light of his phone down over her. 'Oh my God, your feet.'

She knew they wouldn't be a pretty sight, but the swollen, bruised mess they were in shocked her too. 'They're a bit sore.'

'Really? You surprise me.' Grant stood up and loomed over her. 'Paul can walk, can't you?'

'Of course.' A trace of the teenage boy's cockiness returned.

'Good. I'll carry Lila.' Before she

could argue, he swung her up into his arms. 'Paul, pick up our coats and let's go.'

Lila wasn't a woman to easily give in, but she did now, clinging to Grant's neck and allowing him to take care of her.

10

Grant stretched out in the comfy armchair and made short work of the large glass of whisky Nick passed over to him. The moment he'd set foot back in Port Carne, everything became a blur of activity, and the fog was only now clearing from his head.

They'd reunited Paul with his relieved parents, who hadn't even realised he was missing. He'd supposedly gone out with the crowd of other sixteen-year-olds he usually hung around the village with. Grant guessed the boy would be on a short leash for a while after a lecture from the local policeman and a similar one from his father. There'd been no sighting of the Trevear boy, who'd plainly gone to ground until the fuss died down.

Edith bustled into the room, her face wreathed in a broad smile. 'Lila's doing all right and the doctor's gone. She told him she weren't going to hospital on Christmas Eve.'

'If he's a wise man, he didn't argue.' Grant's dry response made everyone laugh.

'I promised him we'd take good care of her. He wants her to stay off her feet as much as possible for at least twenty-four hours. Lila tried to wheedle around him and negotiate going to church tonight, but he swore he'd have her in an ambulance headed for Treliske if she dared to try.'

Grant chuckled. He could smile now, but he hadn't when they'd got back here safely and he'd seen the full extent of her injuries. Badly scraped hands, broken fingernails, a scratched face from the falling gravel — those all paled next to her feet that'd borne the brunt of the taxing climb.

'She wants to come downstairs. Lila says she hates being poked away with no one to talk to. I told her we'd take turns sitting with her, but . . . '

He jumped up. 'Any problem if I carry her down here so she can lie on the sofa instead?'

'I suppose not.'

'I'll do it,' Nick declared. 'You've had a rough evening. Sit down and rest.'

'I'll go,' he insisted, and by the way the whole family stared at him Grant guessed he'd sounded overly brusque. 'Sorry. I didn't mean to be rude.'

'That's okay, mate.' Nick stepped out of the way. 'I know you're worried about her.'

Grant's throat tightened. Worried didn't begin to cover it. Something far more than rescuing a careless teenage boy had happened on the cliff tonight, and it'd take some thinking through. Lila's determination to make her own choices stuck with him, repeating itself on a loop through his head. That was something he needed to come to terms with.

He hurried out of the room but hesitated at the top of the stairs before tapping on her door.

'Come on in.'

'It's only me.' He strolled in, instantly taking a swift check over Lila to see how she looked now. Her high-necked old-fashioned white nightdress emphasised her pale skin, a large plaster adorned her forehead, and her hands were bandaged, but to him she still looked incredibly beautiful.

'Hallo, only you.' She patted the bed. 'Thank heavens you've come to rescue me. I'm goin' stir-crazy here on my own.'

'It's only been,' he said as he checked his watch, 'ten minutes since the esteemed doctor left. Not long enough for even you to wilt from a lack of company.'

'How's Paul?' Lila frowned.

'He's good. Honestly. Thanks to you.' Grant fought to control his emotions.

'What about you?' She leaned closer and touched her bandaged fingers to his chin, forcing him to meet her worried gaze.

Grant shrugged and blinked away the

tears clouding his vision.

'Can you forgive me?'

Her question touched him deep inside, and he hated that she'd had to ask. 'What for? Being a brave, courageous woman? Never apologise for that.'

'But you tried to stop me.' Lila's puzzlement showed, and he struggled to explain.

'The man who . . . cares for you did, but the one who admires your gutsy character realised it was a lost cause.'

'We've got a lot to talk about, haven't we?'

'You could say that,' Grant admitted. 'Right now I'd better take you downstairs or Edith will be on my case.'

She threw off the covers and pointed to a pretty cornflower-blue dressing gown draped over the chair. 'Pass that to me, please.'

'Do you want any help getting it on?'

The scathing glance she tossed his way told Grant she'd be back to her old self very soon.

'Okay. You're not helpless.'

'Quite right.' She wriggled her arms into the flimsy garment and winced, but he held his tongue.

'Ready?'

'I sure am.'

Grant tenderly scooped her into his arms and caught her quick intake of breath.

'Don't fret. I'm not made of porcelain. A few scratches aren't goin' to finish me off.'

They both knew her injuries were far more serious than that, but he played along. 'Come on. Time to hang up your stocking.'

*   *   *

Lila took a cautious sip of her steaming hot mug of tea before setting it back down on the table. She picked up yet another mince pie. Warm, and dripping melting clotted cream down over her hand, they were heaven wrapped up in delicate flaky pastry. Talk about being spoiled. 'It's gone ten o'clock. Y'all need to be getting ready for church soon.' Before Edith could argue, Lila rushed on. 'Nobody is missing the Christmas Eve service for my sake. I'm good to lie here for an hour while you're gone. And Sir Galahad here — ' She pointed at Grant. ' — can whisk me back to bed when you return.'

'I'm staying.' His firm statement came accompanied by a fierce stare.

'Nope, you're not.'

'I am.'

John Warren hauled himself to his feet. 'Hopefully I can still squeeze into my suit for its once-a-year outing.' He headed upstairs, and Lila found herself on the receiving end of one of Ethel's shrewd looks.

'I don't suppose you'll come to any harm, and if you manage to get rid of this one — ' She nodded towards Grant. ' — I'll eat my woolly hat.'

'You might've met your match, Lila. Good luck.' Nick chuckled and ambled off to leave them alone.

Silence descended on the room, broken only by the crackling fire and the slow, gentle tick of the antique brass clock on the mantel.

'Nick's right,' Grant whispered, and Lila turned to face him. In the half-light from the two small lamps burning either side of the sofa, his eyes shone, dark and unfathomable.

Had she met her match? And were they talking about a Christmas Eve carol service, or far more?

'Do you want me to go?' His slow, measured words seeped into Lila's consciousness. 'If you can honestly answer yes, I'll do what you ask.' He leaned forward, resting his hands on his knees. 'But I won't be happy.'

A lone tear trickled down her face and she angrily brushed it away.

In an instant he fell down on his knees in front of her, gently holding her injured hands. 'Oh, Lila, I didn't mean to upset you. Forgive me.'

'What for? Being a strong, caring, protective man? Never apologise for

106

that.' She was paraphrasing his earlier words, and the ghost of a smile tugged at his mouth. 'I guess it's all overwhelmed me and I'm still trying to process it.' She pressed a soft kiss on his cheek. 'Stay with me.'

'You're sure?'

'Very.'

'We could listen to some carols on the radio, if you like.'

Lila nodded. 'I would like. Very much.' *I like everything about being around you, Grant Hawkins.* She pushed her guilt over Belle firmly away.

An hour later, all was peaceful; and with the King's College Choir singing in the background, Lila fell into a sleepy half-doze with her head drooping on Grant's shoulder. He'd shifted to sit on the sofa with her, letting her rest against him with her legs propped up on soft cushions.

'Do you remember what we were talking about when Paul did his screaming thing?' Lila murmured. 'My next question would've been where's your father now, and why aren't you spending Christmas with him when he's all the family you've got?'

'You don't mince words, do you?'

Lila shifted around to see his reaction. 'You called me brave, courageous, and gutsy earlier.' Her reminder drew a smile from him. 'Would you prefer to change that to blunt and tactless now?'

'No.' His resigned sigh amused her. 'My mum and dad both grew up in the Lake District and I was born in Kendall. After she died, he couldn't bear to stay, so we moved almost immediately. He worked a whole slew of temporary jobs from then on, so we never settled anywhere. I probably went to seven or eight different schools over the next ten years.'

'Leaving you always the new kid and struggling to fit in. Been there, done that myself.' Lila shrugged. 'I'm an army brat and we shifted every couple of years. But there were always a bunch of kids in the same situation, so it wasn't the same.'

'Dad's living in Edinburgh at the moment, but I'm sure it won't last much longer. He's been there fifteen months, so he'll be getting itchy feet.'

Underneath Grant's bland explanations, Lila sensed a deep longing for stability.

'Hey, don't you go feeling sorry for me.' He stared into her eyes. 'We don't argue. We just don't . . . stay in touch a lot.'

'But you'll ring him tomorrow?' Lila persisted.

'Maybe.'

'When did you last see him?'

Grant frowned. 'About five years ago. Belle insisted on us going to Manchester so she could meet him. It didn't go well.'

'You mean he didn't come to your wedding or to be with you when you lost Belle?'

'No.' His stony expression darkened.

Lila couldn't imagine a parent not being there for their child when they most needed support, and she struggled to come up with the right thing to say.

Grant tenderly smoothed a stray lock of hair away from her face. 'It's not worth getting upset about. It is what it is,' he said firmly, and glanced away. 'Hey, do you realise the time?'

Lila checked her watch. 'It's nearly midnight.'

'I've an idea.' He shifted her gently so he could stand up, then went over to the stereo and sorted through the Warrens' CD collection. 'This will work.' He fiddled around, and soon the strains of 'Silent Night' filled the room. Taking two white candles out of Edith's mantel decorations, he handed one to Lila. 'Matches. There must be some around here.' He disappeared into the kitchen and she heard him rifling through the drawers and cupboards.

'Success.' He returned brandishing a cigarette lighter, then lit both candles and turned off the lamps so only the flickering candles glowed between them. Perching on the arm of the sofa, he started to sing, and Lila haltingly joined in. The timeless words sent a wave of emotion coursing through her, and she fought to continue through her tears. The music stopped, and in the silence the church bells chimed the hour.

'Happy Christmas,' Grant said.

'Merry Christmas to you too,' Lila whispered and tilted her face up to him, ready for his kiss. But Grant drew away. He stood up to turn all the lights back on and blew out their candles.

'I'll get you settled upstairs before everyone comes home. You ought to rest.'

Lila nodded and didn't argue.

11

Grant stood in the garden and watched the glowing sun begin its slow rise over today's flat silver-blue sea. He'd given up trying to sleep when his brain refused to quieten down. Between rehashing last night's dramatic rescue and his thought-provoking conversations with Lila, he'd been too worn out to rest.

What he struggled to work out was how in a few short days she'd burrowed under his skin and wriggled her way into a vacant corner of his heart. Close behind in his musings came the Warren family and Port Carne. Over the last three years, he'd trained himself to forget how much they meant to him, and he'd made a conscious decision to stay away. Instead of allowing them to help him grieve and find a way to reshape his life, he'd blotted them out.

I can't stay here, son. Your mother's in every inch of this place. It'll be easier for us both.

His father's words, spoken a mere three weeks after they lost Grant's mother, haunted him still, and yet he'd still foolishly copied Ian Hawkins's terrible example. Going for his usual run in a minute would either exhaust him enough to go back to bed and finally get some sleep, or at least pass the time until someone else woke up.

'Seriously, mate?' Nick stood at the back door, staring at Grant's running shoes and shaking his head. 'Are you ready for heroic rescue number two?'

'Don't be daft. I don't intend to stop running there because of a couple of stupid teenagers.' Grant became aware of the dark shadows under his old friend's eyes. 'What're you doing up this early? I didn't think sunrises were your thing.' At university he'd often dragged Nick out of bed in time for lectures. 'Everything all right?'

'I suppose so.' He paced around the

tiny patio, barely avoiding bumping into the chairs in his agitation. Usually this would be the point in their conversations where Grant would crack a joke or change the subject. Lila must be affecting him. 'What's up? I can tell something's bothering you.'

'My God, just because Lila's a typical American and got you blabbing about your feelings, don't try pulling the same trick on me,' Nick retorted.

'Don't be unkind. She's a good woman.' Grant ignored his friend's dramatic eye-roll. 'I'm sorry for trying to help. I'll leave you to wallow in self-pity, because we all know that works wonders.' He picked up his empty tea mug from the table. 'See you later.'

'Maybe I'll come with you. It might do me good.'

Walking with Lila last night put multiple cracks in his own shell, so maybe it'd do the same for Nick. 'Feel free.'

'Give me five minutes to change.'

'Might be best.' He smiled at Nick's snowman-design sleep shorts and matching T-shirt. 'Last year's Christmas present? Bit cold for those today out on the cliffs.'

'Very funny,' Nick snapped and strode off, plainly angry about a lot more than Grant's warped sense of humour.

He started his leg stretches and shook out his arms, the muscles still strained from the long distance he'd carried Lila last night.

'Okay. Torture me,' Nick dragged back out, not exactly brimming with enthusiasm.

'We'll start off slow. I'm guessing you haven't run in a while?' The only response to his question was another glare.

Grant jogged along the road and gradually picked up speed as he headed along the steep path towards the cliffs. Occasionally he glanced behind to make sure Nick was in sight, but otherwise gave himself up to enjoying the crisp, clear morning.

'Any chance of a breather?' Nick

gasped, and without waiting for an answer dropped down onto the grass. 'How the heck you do this every morning is beyond me. You must be mad.'

Grant joined him and wondered how honest to be. 'The opposite, really. If I don't run most days, that's when the crazies return. After I lost Belle, I basically fell apart, and this saved me.' He leaned back and propped himself up on his hands. The hypnotic rhythm of the waves bumping up against the rocks and the occasional squawk of a gull flying over them helped Grant to be patient.

'My firm's offered me a job in New Zealand. A big promotion. Opening a new office in Auckland,' Nick blurted out.

'That's great. You'll love it. It's supposed to be a beautiful country. I'd like to get there myself one day. What's the problem?'

'Mainly my dad. He's working too hard, and the doctor recommended he took things easier.'

'Okay.' Grant still didn't see the connection. 'You're worried about leaving your parents? Wouldn't they see it's a great opportunity for you? It doesn't have to be forever, and surely they could get some help in the shop?'

Nick shoved a hand through his thick blond hair. 'I should've known *you* wouldn't get it. You don't *do* family, do you? You about broke Belle's heart when you told her you didn't want kids.'

'I never said that exactly,' he protested. 'I wasn't ready that's all.'

'Come on, we both know your situation. It's messed you up.'

Grant was speechless. Everyone else appeared to have seen it apart from him.

'My dad took over the hardware shop from his father, and he's always expected I'd do the same one day,' Nick said.

'But you're an accountant.'

Nick clutched his bent knees and

stared off into the distance. 'I've never spelled out that I absolutely wouldn't want to run the business. I suppose he assumed I'd come around.'

'You really want this New Zealand job, don't you?'

'Yep, I do.'

'I'll think on it. Maybe I'll have a brainwave.'

'Thanks.' Nick managed a brief smile. 'You're not bad, as mates go.'

Grant jumped back up. 'Get your lazy bones moving. We're almost half-way, and we need to work off all the turkey and Christmas pudding your mother's at home cooking right now.' Instead of sorting out his own confused thoughts, he'd added another problem to the mix.

* * *

Lila added Grant's present to the pile under the Christmas tree and limped back out into the hall. With any luck, she could sneak back upstairs before anyone spotted her.

'What're you doing out of bed?' Grant's stern voice startled her, and she turned to see him lurking by the kitchen door. 'Shall I call the doctor and tell him you're disobeying his orders?'

'Merry Christmas to you too, Mr. Scrooge.' His severe expression cracked into a broad smile and she bathed in the glow.

'I gather you're feeling better?'

'Much. I slept all night, and Edith brought me enough breakfast to feed a family of four. She stood over me until I finished it all.' Lila tried not to be aware of his nearness but failed miserably, picking up on a delicious hint of rich woodsy cologne hanging around him this morning. 'How are you?'

'Good. Nick and I went for a run earlier on.'

'Back to the scene of the crime?' she teased.

'Yes. Edith's had a reporter from the local newspaper on the phone. They wanted to interview us, but she put a flea in their ear and told them to ring back tomorrow.'

Lila shuddered. 'I'm not interested in being plastered over the front page, thank you very much.'

'Me neither.'

She'd read enough news stories online after Belle's tragic death to guess that any media attention would horrify Grant.

'I can't believe I just noticed today's fashion statement.' He pointed to her jumper. 'Did you bring a suitcase full of the things?'

'Don't be rude.' She pulled herself up to her full five feet six inches and straightened her shoulders. 'They're festive.'

'Oh, they're that all right.' Grant chuckled. 'Do these ring?' He tugged on one of the silver bells hanging from Rudolph's neck. 'Sweet.'

'I'm going back to my room and do my make-up.'

'Why? You're beautiful without any.'

A hot red flush lit up his face and neck. 'Sorry, I didn't — '

'Didn't mean it? I hope that's not what you were going to say, because that *would* be rude.' Lila loved how easily she could tie him up in verbal knots. 'I'll see you in a little while.' She instantly guessed Grant's intention as she crossed the hall. 'I can walk. Don't even . . . '

Grant scooped her off her feet before she finished the sentence. 'Remember what the doctor said.'

Lila gave in and wrapped her hands around the back of his neck where his soft springy hair tickled her fingers.

'I'd appreciate your advice later about something Nick told me.' He easily carried her up the short flight of stairs and lowered her down on her feet outside the bedroom door.

'Playing agony uncle now, are you?'

He frowned. 'Sort of. Not my thing, but he . . . talked and . . . '

'You tried listening for a change.' Lila's succinct summing-up made him

121

wince. She took advantage and kissed his cheek. 'Well done.'

'I'll be back to take you down for coffee and presents in an hour or so.' Grant's blunt statement made her smile. 'Put your feet up until then.'

'Yes, sir, I sure will.'

'Liar. You'll fiddle around doing your face. Make phone calls. Hang out of the window to check the weather. When you hear me coming up the stairs, you'll hop on the bed and pretend you've been there all the time.'

She tossed her head in the air and stuck out her tongue before disappearing into her room, with his loud unrestrained laughter ringing in her ears. The man understood her far too well. She'd get her own back later.

12

Grant met the unmistakeable challenge in Lila's sparkling eyes. 'I couldn't leave it in the shop, could I?' she said.

Yes, you really could have. If he wore this jumper with its bloated Father Christmas face, manic grin and straggly beard, he'd resemble a fat mouldy tomato. 'I'm pretty sure it isn't large enough.'

'Try it on.'

'Yes, try it on, mate,' Nick echoed.

If it wasn't Christmas Day, he'd wipe the smirk off his friend's face in short order. Edith joined in the encouragement while John simply sat back and laughed. Grant pulled his navy-blue jumper over his head and tossed it to one side. At least his white T-shirt would prevent too much of the fuzzy, itchy-looking wool from touching his skin.

'It was a bargain. Only five pounds in the charity shop,' Lila said.

Wonderful. Someone else's rejected clothes.

'Edith washed it for you. It's clean,' she assured him.

'How reassuring. Thank you, Edith.' His sarcasm made both women blush. Grant didn't have any choice, so he yanked on the ugly jumper. He tugged the sleeves down and straightened out the front to better show off the gaudy design.

'Wow, it fits perfectly,' Lila exclaimed.

'You'll have to wear it down the pub tonight,' Nick insisted. If they weren't in mixed company, Grant would tell him exactly what he thought of the appalling idea. If his old friend thought he'd be seen in public wearing this, he could think again.

'Great idea.' Lila giggled. 'We'll all go down and show off our Christmas sweaters.'

'What a pity I don't have one. Sorry about that.' Nick grinned.

'No problem.' Lily pointed to a large silver-wrapped box. 'That's from me.'

Nick's dubious expression changed to outright horror as he revealed the contents.

Grant roared with laughter. 'Try it on, mate,' he parroted his friend's words back at him. Like a man preparing for his execution, Nick pulled the offending garment on over his check shirt. 'I thought mine was bad.'

'There wasn't much choice,' Lila protested. 'With Nick's blond hair, I thought the angel would suit him better than you.'

He could've kissed her. At least his ugly jumper didn't boast an oversized angel with a gaudy gold halo and a tinsel wand. *Be grateful for small mercies.*

'I think we've all done very well,' Edith declared. 'I love my perfume, Lila, and you've made the boys look very . . . handsome. I'm sure the whisky will help to soften things.' She stifled a giggle.

'I'm sorry, I didn't get around to putting my presents under the tree.' Grant fished inside the plastic carrier bag he'd brought in from the cottage and passed out small badly wrapped packages to Edith, John and Nick. 'I made these myself, but I didn't know you'd be here, Lila, so I bought this for you yesterday.' He passed her a small black velvet box, overtaken by a sudden wave of nerves. 'I didn't have any wrapping paper.' As she opened the lid, he rushed to explain. 'It's for your hair. Celtic knots.' He'd spotted it in the window of a small jeweller's shop and known the mass of shimmering silver knots would be perfect for her ponytail.

'Oh, Grant, it's beautiful.' Lila glanced up at him with shining eyes.

No, you're the beautiful one. He caught Edith's wistful smile, and a wave of guilt swamped him. God, he was stupid. The gift was too personal, and it wasn't the right time or place.

'It's very pretty, dear. Put it on,' Edith urged. In a strange way, Grant sensed she'd bestowed a sort of blessing on them. He took it as an encouragement to him not to feel guilty about going on with his life.

Lila untied the red bow she'd been wearing, and he watched in fascination as she shook out her hair, sleeked it down with her fingers and scooped up a neat ponytail. With a flick of her wrist, she fixed the silver ornament in place.

'It's time I put the potatoes in the oven.' Edith disappeared into the kitchen.

'I didn't know you could make anything this good.' Nick held up an intricate wooden puzzle fitted together to form the shape of a box.

'You could be more tactful, son,' John implored as he studied his own gift. His was a straightforward box decorated with a selection of inlaid woods, engraved with his initials and designed to hold a deck of playing cards.

'I assume you still play poker every week?' Grant said.

'I do indeed. That's a nice piece of

work.' He smoothed his fingers over the wood.

'Wow, let me see.' Lila took the box from John. 'Do you sell these?'

'No, don't be daft,' Grant answered. 'I make them for my own amusement. Gives me something to do in the evenings.'

'Hmm, we'll discuss that later.'

He knew what that meant — she'd add it to the list of 'things you need to talk about'.

* * *

Out of the blue, Lila's confidence wavered. They were managing to enjoy the day so far, but tomorrow — the third anniversary of Belle's death — would be a different story. If Lila had been more forceful, and made the phone call she should've made, would everything be different? Grant certainly wouldn't be buying pretty silver ties for her hair and smiling indulgently at her across the room.

'I'm a little tired. I think I'll have a rest before we eat.' That wasn't a complete lie. Her feet were sore, and it'd feel good to stretch out on the bed.

'I'll take you.' Grant immediately jumped up.

Upstairs, he set her down gently and opened her bedroom door. 'I'll provide another human taxi service when Edith gives me my orders.'

'Thanks for everything.' Lila tried to convey how much she appreciated his caring, but stopped there, not daring to go on.

'Is everything okay?' He rested his hand on her arm, and for a second she almost told him everything. But the idea of losing his admiration or the generosity of the Warrens towards her made Lila hold her tongue. 'Yeah. I'm tired, that's all.'

'We'll discuss it later.' Grant threw her earlier words right back at her, and all she could do was to turn away and leave him standing there.

Before she did anything else, Lila

went into the bathroom, grabbed her hand mirror and turned to check out the back of her head. The dangling silver knots sparkled in the light, and the idea that Grant had scoured the crowded shops yesterday for something that would please her brought tears to her eyes.

He's such a special man, Lila. I don't want to worry him if it's not necessary. I just needed to confide in someone, and you've always been there for me. Promise me you won't say anything.

Belle's last e-mails haunted her. In the bedroom, she pulled her suitcase out from under the bed and retrieved the bundle of printed messages. She'd considered showing them to Edith and John, not from any expectation of forgiveness but simply to give them the full story. But as soon as they met, she'd known she couldn't follow through. She needed to come to terms with her conscience alone without hurting the Warrens any further in the process.

She'd planned on staying all the way

through the New Year, but would make an excuse to leave earlier. She wouldn't actually start work on revamping the window displays of their flagship London shop until after the Christmas sales, but she could pretend they needed her for discussions at the headquarters office.

Lila shoved the papers away again. For now she'd prove she didn't always tell lies by lying down and at least attempting to take a nap.

From somewhere, a banging noise penetrated her fuzzy head, and she sat up in the bed.

'This is your personal dinner gong.' Grant's deep, rich voice sneaked into the room and she couldn't help smiling. A few days ago he'd arrived here tired, withdrawn, and quiet, and now what a difference there was. She didn't believe for a minute that his transformation was all down to her; being surrounded by people who cared for him and Cornwall itself had helped to work some magic.

'Give me five minutes,' she said.

'Are those female minutes or regular clock ones?' he teased. 'Punctuality wasn't Belle's strong point, and her minutes were exceedingly elastic.'

'I know, but remember I grew up with an army officer father. If we weren't ready at least two minutes early for everything, we'd be in trouble.'

'My apologies.'

Through the door she sensed him smile. Lila freshened up and changed into a red long-sleeved T-shirt covered in silver snowflakes. She added a slick of glossy red lipstick and hurried to open the door. 'Four minutes and twenty seconds.'

'Impressive.' He checked her out. 'How do you get to ditch the ugly sweater?'

'I was too hot, plus I'm a woman, and we're allowed to change our minds along with our clothes.' Lila's pert response brought out another of his glorious smiles.

'You certainly are.' He swept her off

her feet, laughing when she gasped at his swift move. 'After you've eaten all the food Edith's got ready, I might struggle to carry you back up here.'

She playfully smacked his back. 'Rude man.'

'Never.' He refused to put her down until they reached the dining room.

'I feel terrible not being able to help,' she complained.

'Don't worry, Edith's got everything under control and John's been her assistant. Nick's seeing to the drinks, and they landed me with the job of laying the table.'

Lila noticed the inexpertly folded napkins and uneven tablecloth, short on one side and draping down to the floor on the other.

'I know it's lame, but it's the best I could manage,' Grant said.

'Move the flowers and the candles out of the way.' She couldn't tolerate looking at this disaster all the way through the meal.

'But . . .'

'No buts. I'm fine.' Once he'd done as she asked, Lila straightened the cloth before starting on the napkins. Soon each plate boasted an intricately shaped swan, and she prepared to tackle the decorations. She placed the poinsettia back in the middle of the table and frowned.

'What's wrong? Stick the candles back on and we're good.'

'It's dull.'

'If you say so.' Grant pulled out a chair and sat down. 'I'll watch.'

'Best thing you can do,' Lila quipped. She poked around in Edith's sideboard and discovered several crystal vases, a few small gold-coloured dishes, and a simple wooden Christmas tree pushed all the way to the back. 'Fetch the fruit bowl from the other room and the bowl of nuts.'

'Sure you wouldn't like the kitchen sink while we're at it?' he half-heartedly groused, and left to do her bidding.

Ten minutes later, Lila folded her arms and smiled. She'd set the poinsettia back on the sideboard out of the way and made the Christmas tree the focal point of the table. Tangerines glowed in the glass vases, the gold dishes were heaped with nuts, and a selection of white and gold candles gleamed, bringing the table and the room to life.

'You're good,' Grant said.

Edith hurried in, carrying a vegetable dish in each hand, and came to an abrupt halt. All the colour leached from her face, and she swayed on her feet. 'Belle's tree. Where did you find it?' Her husky voice throbbed with pain, and Lila wished a hole would open up and swallow her alive.

13

'I'll take those.' Grant eased the dishes from Edith's hands and set them on the table. He pulled out a chair and encouraged her to sit down. 'Lila took pity on my sad efforts with the table. I'm sorry if we've used something we shouldn't.'

'Real sorry,' Lila whispered. 'The last thing I'd ever want to do is to hurt y'all.'

Edith reached out and picked up the tree, cradling it in her hands. 'Belle made this when she were about eight. They did them at school and she gave it to me for Christmas. For years she always put it right where you did.'

'I found it stuck in the back behind a pile of napkins.' Lila pointed to the sideboard. 'It never occurred to me . . .'

'No reason why it should, my 'andsome. When Belle got a bit older, she said it was stupid, and I wasn't to use it anymore and embarrass her.' Edith cracked a smile. 'I bet she hid it so I wouldn't be tempted to take it out again.'

'I'll put it away,' Lila offered.

'No. Don't you dare. I want it to stay there.'

'I agree,' John spoke up. 'That's its rightful place.'

A tight knot formed in Grant's throat. Some might consider this to be the downside of coming here, but being surrounded by all the other people who'd loved Belle eased the solitary grief he'd lived with for far too long.

'Our lunch will be ruined in a minute,' Edith declared, returning to her usual brisk self. 'John, come and bring the rest of the food in. Nick, pour us all a drink for goodness sake. And you two — ' She glanced at Grant and Lila. ' — wait there and get ready to eat.'

Grant touched Lila's shoulder, desperate to say the right thing and bring some warmth back to her face. 'Sit by me so I can tell you what everything is.'

She raised her eyebrows. 'Why? I thought a turkey was a turkey, or are Cornish ones hugely different?'

'Our turkeys are the same, but do you have bacon-wrapped chipolatas and stuffing balls? What about setting fire to a pudding for dessert?'

Lila tossed up her hands in mock-submission. 'You've gotten me officially bewildered. I give in. I'll let you be my culinary guide to all things Christmas where Cornwall is concerned.'

'Good girl.'

'Thanks,' she murmured. 'You're a good man.' Lila gave him a quick hug, and a drift of warm floral perfume surrounded him.

Nick strolled in, brandishing two wine bottles. 'Red or white?'

Grant caught a hint of disappointment in Lila's eyes and gave her hand a surreptitious squeeze under the table. Hopefully she'd realise they weren't done.

An hour later, everyone stopped

eating and admitted defeat. Grant suspected he wouldn't be capable of moving again this side of midnight, but that didn't matter. He'd been right to come here, and one day he'd be able to thank Nick properly. He'd spent the last two Christmases alone and survived by treating them the same as any other day, staying busy in his workshop before throwing a frozen dinner into the microwave at supper time.

'I know you'd all help clear away, but John knows my routine. We'll get it done quicker on our own and be ready to listen to the Queen at three o'clock.' Edith stood up. 'Take a walk, make your phone calls or go on that Facebook thing until we're cleared away.'

'What's your choice?' Grant asked Lila.

'I'm going to call home. They should all be awake by now, so I'll catch them before the worst of the chaos starts.' She gave him a shrewd stare. 'Are you going to phone your dad?'

'Maybe later. I might go for a walk.'

139

He glanced down over himself and grimaced. 'After I've changed. I don't want to frighten the natives.'

Lila pouted. 'You're hurtin' my feelings now. I chose that 'specially for you. Some people don't appreciate good taste.'

'They certainly don't. I'm keeping mine on,' Nick boasted with a silly grin.

'How many glasses of wine did you have?' Grant said. 'You need your head examined.'

'Go on. Off with you.' Lila shooed him away. 'I'll see you later.'

He wanted to say so much, but yet again it wasn't the right time or place.

'Don't fret. I'm not mad. That's not my style.' Lily pulled out her phone and headed for the door, before glancing back over her shoulder and winking. 'I'll get even instead.'

Nick gave Grant a strange look as Lila left them alone.

'Is something up, mate?' Grant challenged.

'You tell me.'

'It's nothing important.'

'You don't think so?' Nick persisted.

'It's confusing.'

'Women always are — haven't you worked that one out yet?' Nick's smile faded. 'Sorry. That was tactless. You didn't expect to go through all this again, did you?'

'No.' Grant didn't pretend to misunderstand. 'I never did the whole 'is she/isn't she interested/what's my next move' thing well.'

'Don't look to me for advice. I'm pretty much a failure when it comes to anything long-term, and I don't know why,' Nick admitted.

'Maybe there's a Kiwi girl's heart with your name on it.'

'Not likely to find out, am I?'

His morose reply struck Grant hard, and he struggled to come up with a cheering response.

'Hey, no worries. I'll leave you to it. I'm going to try and crack that fiendish puzzle.' He disappeared, leaving Grant alone and wondering what to do next.

* ★ ★

'It's hard, Mom.' Lila sighed, wishing she could be totally honest. There weren't many things she'd kept a secret from her mother, but her part in Belle's tragic death was the biggest. 'I'm not sure if I've made things worse by being here.' Mary Beth Caswell didn't pull any punches, and Lila spent the next few minutes being reprimanded. Everything her mother said made sense but still left her wondering. 'Grant's here, too — Belle's husband.'

After a few minutes of casual conversation, Mary Beth pounced. 'Be careful, sweetheart.'

'In what way?'

'Don't play me for a fool,' Mary Beth scoffed. 'I gave birth to you and I know you better than anyone else. Who guessed about your first crush on little Bobby Manning next door when you were ten years old? Answer me two questions. Is Grant interested in you too, and is he ready to date again?'

'Yeah, he's attracted to me. I'd have to say probably a big fat no to your second question.'

'But part of him wants to give it a try, and so do you?'

'I guess.'

'You're there for a few weeks. Maybe that'll be enough time to get to know each other better and see what happens.'

Lila thought longingly of her return train ticket to London. Using it sooner rather than later might be a smart move. 'Maybe.'

'Don't rush into anything. I don't want you to get hurt.'

Me neither, but most of all I don't want to hurt Grant. He's been through enough. 'I'll be OK. Promise.' *At least until he looks at me with those vivid green eyes and touches my cheek so gently I could cry.* 'I'd better go. Edith's calling me to say she's got tea ready, and you know what the Brits are like about their tea. I'll be in trouble if I don't hurry up.' She quickly said goodbye and hung up.

So much for not lying again. She hadn't heard Edith at all, but she couldn't take more of her mother's wise advice.

Grant knocked. 'It's only me. I know it's early, but I thought you might be at a loose end.'

She opened the door and smiled right back at him. That could be something to do with the appalling jumper he wore with such charm. 'I thought you were abandoning your new present to go for a walk?'

'I changed my mind.' He patted the distorted Father Christmas face and grinned. 'Couldn't bear to be parted from him.'

'I'm glad you're coming around to the virtues of the ugly Christmas sweater.'

Grant leaned against the doorframe. 'After we have the obligatory cup of tea, could we sneak outside? I don't think it's too cold to sit on the patio for a while. I'd like to talk about Nick . . . and a few other things.'

Lila pretended to shake out her ears.

'Did I hear you right? For a second there I thought you said you wanted to talk.'

'Okay, very funny.' He laughed. 'Is that a — '

'It's a not-date. Remember we're avoiding that word.'

'Oh, I remember.'

'Fine. Are you going to do your strong-man act again?' She caught his quick intake of breath. 'Just for today. Tomorrow morning I'll have had enough of being feeble.'

Grant easily swept her up into his arms, and for a few seconds she rested her head on his shoulder. 'I'm not looking forward to tomorrow,' he murmured. 'I *need* to go down to the beach, although I don't want to. I wondered if you'd come with me.'

Lila wished herself a million miles away.

'Sorry. I shouldn't have asked. Forget I said anything.'

'I can't.'

'Can't come or can't forget?'

'Both,' she sighed. 'Put me down.'

'Why?'

'Because there's something I need to show you.' It'd been his question with its clear implication of trust that'd made up her mind. She'd lived with this awful burden for three years and couldn't do it for another minute. If this meant losing his respect, and along with that the chance of love, so be it.

'Okay.' He frowned and set her back on her feet. He waited in silence while she opened the bedroom door.

'Sit down.' Lila pointed to the old wicker chair and went about getting the sheaf of papers back out. She perched on the edge of the bed close to him. 'I'm going to tell you a few things first, and then you can read these. But I want you to know that I don't expect your forgiveness.'

'Stop there,' Grant pleaded. 'I don't want to hear this.'

'You have to.' Before she lost her nerve, Lila began to recite the whole sad story.

146

14

Grant couldn't get his head around Lila's words. No matter which way he looked at it, she'd lied. Worst of all was the crippling knowledge that she could possibly have saved Belle. 'Let me get this perfectly clear.' He kept his anger in check by adopting a cold, dispassionate tone. 'Belle confessed to you that she'd been having heart palpitations and shortness of breath. She also mentioned being born with a hole in the heart — a condition that was left to close on its own but left her more vulnerable to heart problems as an adult. You were aware she'd made a doctor's appointment to discuss these problems, but that she still planned to do the Boxing Day Polar Bear Plunge.'

'Yes. That's all true. And I did nothing.' Lila's head drooped into her hands.

'Why?' he pleaded, desperate to understand her rationale.

'Because she asked me not to, and I thought — '

'You *thought*,' Grant yelled and jumped to his feet. 'That's the last thing you did.' He planted himself in front of her, touching her chin and forcing her to look at him. 'If for one second, just one second, you really *had* thought, you'd have known some promises are meant to be broken. For a person's own safety. To save their life.' Lila flinched, and he squashed down the urge to retract his harsh words.

'Take them.' She forced the stack of emails into his hands.

'Were you seriously going to show these to Belle's parents?'

Lila shrugged. 'I thought it might be the right thing to do, but after I met them I realised I'd only be doing it to salve my own conscience.' She hesitated. 'Of course I could be wrong about that too. I'll leave it up to you to decide whether or not to tell them.'

'Thanks a bunch. Land it on me.'

'For what it's worth, I'm sorry.'

Grant scoffed. 'You're too late.'

'I know,' she whispered. 'If you don't mind, could you tell Edith I'm too tired to come down again and that I've gone to bed? I'll make an excuse to leave in the morning.'

'But she'll — '

'I'm good at lying when I have to be. You know that now.' The wistful trace of a smile tugged at her lips. 'I'll make it sound good.'

'I'm sure you will.' Grant's stiff reply made her wince. He couldn't stay in the same room with Lila any longer. As he stalked out, the urge to slam the door almost overwhelmed him, but he stamped it down. Drawing attention to themselves was the last thing they needed.

He crept downstairs and sneaked out of the back door to the guest cottage. At least there he could fall apart in peace. Lila had pushed him back to the same bitter place it'd taken him so long to climb out of, and destroyed the budding relationship between them with a few choice words. So much for a happy Christmas.

Lila gripped the bedcover to keep herself from running after him. The same question ran in a continuous loop around her head. If Grant hadn't asked her to go with him in the morning to the beach, would she still have told him everything? Probably not. She'd always been convinced it'd be a relief to share her guilty secret; but instead a bleak, hollow emptiness swept through her. She curled up on the bed, hugged her pillow, and closed her eyes to blot out the picture of Grant's sorrowful eyes staring at her in disbelief.

A light tapping noise disturbed her, and she struggled to focus on her bedside clock.

'I brought you some supper, love. It's nearly eight o'clock.' Edith's kind voice brought everything rushing back, and Lila couldn't face her. She crept out of the bed and sneaked into the bathroom.

'Just a sec,' she yelled, anxious to give herself a moment to think. She ran the cold tap and splashed water over her face. A quick glance in the mirror helped to crystallise her decision. She'd use her pathetic appearance to her advantage. Instead of tidying her hair and touching up her smudged make-up, she did the opposite. She undid her ponytail and tossed the silver knot ornament to one side, then rubbed at her eyes to make herself resemble a very sad racoon. Running back into the bedroom, she threw herself on the bed. 'Come in.'

'Here we go. I . . . ' Edith's eyes widened. 'What's up, my 'andsome? Aren't you feeling well?'

There wasn't any need to act, because her tears automatically began to flow. 'I'm sorry.' Lila wiped ineffectually at her face. 'I'm just really tired and a bit homesick, I guess.'

Edith put the tray on top of the dressing table and sat on the bed. 'It won't do you no good to mope up here on your own. Eat a bite of supper, and then I'll get Grant to help you downstairs.'

'No,' Lila snapped. 'Sorry. I didn't mean to be rude. I only meant my feet are okay now. I don't need mollycoddling.'

'I suppose you know what you're about.' Edith fetched the tray and settled it on Lila's lap. 'I've done you a few turkey sandwiches and added a couple of sausage rolls and a pickled onion.' Edith smiled. 'My John always reckons Christmas Day supper isn't complete without one of my pickles.'

The small brown onion in the middle of the plate didn't look very appealing, but the Christmas cake hadn't either, so Lila hoped she'd be proved wrong again.

'When you come down, we'll have a cup of tea and I'll warm up a few mince pies.'

There wouldn't be any escape. She'd have to join the family again or stir up a whole raft of questions she wouldn't be able to answer. Maybe Grant would stay out of the way. *Why should he? You're the one in the wrong.* 'Thanks. You've been so good to me.' *Far more than I deserve.*

Edith patted her hand. 'You were a good friend to my girl, and it's helped us having you here today.'

Tears choked Lila's throat and she couldn't speak.

'We'll see you later, and maybe we'll play some cards. It was always one of our routines, but we haven't done it lately.' Her smile faltered. 'I told myself I wouldn't dwell on things today. That's enough of all that. Don't take any notice of me.' She bustled away before Lila could find something sympathetic to say.

You've done enough harm. Keep quiet.

★   ★   ★

Grant avoided mid-afternoon tea by honestly claiming to be still full from

153

lunch; but when it came to supper, Edith wouldn't listen to his protests and insisted that he joined them. Somehow he ate enough to placate her by forcing down a couple of sausage rolls and a sandwich. He managed to make an appropriately sympathetic response when Edith explained about Lila not feeling well. When he heard she'd probably come down later to play cards, he started to plan his exit strategy.

Are you going to phone your Dad?

He'd evaded Lila's question earlier, but it'd certainly solve his problem and . . . *And what? Please Lila at the same time?* Grant rationalised the decision in his head. Ringing his father twice in one year could hardly be termed excessive, and most people got in touch with their families at Christmas.

'You'll have to excuse me.' Grant plastered on a smile. 'I need to ring my father, and it'll be too late soon if I don't get on with it.' Edith's indulgent smile made him briefly feel guilty. No doubt she'd heard stories from Belle about his difficult relationship with his father and thought some miraculous reconciliation was on the cards. She couldn't be further from the truth, but he wouldn't burst her bubble tonight.

'You run along and make sure to come back for a cup of tea later.'

'Thanks. I'll see how the time's doing.' That made it sound as though he'd be chatting to his father for hours, which was highly unlikely. 'I'll take a piece of cake with me just in case.'

That did the trick, and a few minutes later he made his escape, loaded down with a huge slice of Christmas cake, several mince pies and another thick turkey sandwich. 'In case you get hungry, my love,' Edith has said.

It used to baffle him how Belle took her parents' constant help and concern for granted, but now he understood it came from a place of unshakeable certainty, not indifference. He stopped and hugged Edith, wishing he could explain how much it meant to be included in her circle of caring.

'Don't get soppy on me or I'll be in tears again,' she remonstrated with him, but her gleaming eyes betrayed nothing but pleasure. 'Get on with you.'

Back at the cottage, he wasted time changing clothes and turning on the electric fire to take the chill off of the empty room before turning on his phone. Immediately it vibrated with an incoming call, and he checked the screen.

'Hey, you beat me to it, Dad. Happy Christmas.'

'Don't claim you were just about to ring me. We don't lie to each other, Grant. I always told you the truth whether you liked it or not.' His father's gruff words pushed him right back to childhood. The blunt way Ian dealt with everything after losing his wife had shaped Grant, and not usually for the best. It was no wonder Belle frequently got mad at him for being stoic and uncommunicative.

'It's not a lie. I'm in Cornwall staying

156

with the Warrens, and if you like I'll call Edith in and you can ask her yourself. I've just left them to come and ring you. You can believe it or not. Your choice.' He held his breath.

'Maybe I jumped to conclusions.'

Don't say sorry, will you? No miracles are going to happen. Not this Christmas. 'How are you, anyway?' Grant got the ball rolling. They always went through the same ritual of asking after each other and pretending more interest in the answers than they really felt. After five minutes, one of them would say it'd been good to talk and that they must do it more often. The other would agree, and that would be the extent of their communication for another six months.

'If we're being honest, I'm not too good, son.'

'In what way?'

'I've had a few niggling health problems recently, and they did a load of tests at the hospital last week. I should get the results in a couple of days.'

Grant didn't probe for any more details. 'I hope everything goes well, and let me know how you get on.' He took a chance and kept going. 'I mean that. If I don't hear from you, I'm going to ring again.'

'Fine. I'll call. Don't get antsy.'

Grant decided he imagined the waver in his father's voice. *You tried listening for a change.* Remembering Lila's response when he'd been talking about Nick took his breath away.

'You still there?' his father asked.

'Of course I am.'

'It's tomorrow, isn't it?

For a second, the question didn't register. 'Yes, three years.' It astonished Grant that he'd remembered. When Belle died, his father made one brief phone call, didn't attend the funeral, and never mentioned her again. Thanks to Lila, he recognised Ian's reaction as a deep-seated fear of losing control of his emotions.

'You'll get through it and keep going.'

'Did time help you?' He'd no idea

what made him ask such a deeply personal question. They didn't do this. 'Sorry. Not my business.'

His father sighed. 'No, it is your business. I'm afraid it hasn't, but only because I haven't let it. That's the best answer I can give you. I've got to go now.'

Of course you do. You always move on rather than face things. 'Me too.' Grant refused to give in too easily. 'Remember to ring when you get your test results.'

'I made you a promise. I'm a lot of things, son, and not all of them are good, but I'm not a liar.' Ian abruptly ended the call.

Grant turned off his phone and his gaze caught sight of the pile of emails he'd thrown on the table. He reluctantly picked up the one on the top, knowing he wouldn't sleep until he'd read them all.

15

'I'm sorry about having to leave, but there's a chance I'll make it back for the New Year,' Lila explained. She'd no intention of returning to Cornwall anytime soon, but hoped her little white lie would ease Edith's disappointment. 'I've got to go right away, or I won't make it back to London for tomorrow morning's meeting.' She avoided Nick's shrewd stare, getting the distinct suspicion he wasn't falling for her story. Last night she'd made up her mind to cut short her visit, only to discover there weren't any trains running today because of the Boxing Day holiday. She'd been lucky to snag the last available seat on a coach leaving Truro shortly before eight o'clock this morning and reaching London by mid-afternoon.

'I'll run you up to the bus station,' Nick offered.

'There's no need. I've ordered a taxi.' She checked her watch. 'In fact, it should be here in ten minutes. I'd better get my things.'

'I'll help. You don't need to be carrying a load of stuff down the stairs,' Nick insisted. 'You're still recovering from your injuries, plus you weren't well last night.'

Lila caved in, unable to argue without revealing too much, and thought she'd got away with it until they reached her bedroom.

'So what's up between you and Grant?'

She kept her face turned away and worked on finishing her packing. 'Nothing. Why?'

'You want a list?' He ticked off on his fingers. 'I heard him yelling up here last night. The two of you avoided being downstairs together in the evening. He's always an early riser, but we haven't seen any sign of him this morning, and all of a sudden you're cutting short your visit for a mythical meeting.'

'It's not myth . . . ' Lila couldn't

finish. She sighed and passed her bags over to Nick. 'It's difficult. If Grant wants to tell you, he can.'

'Oh, I'm sure I'll get it out of Mr. Taciturn. He's tighter than a clam when he wants to be.' His bitter sarcasm struck Lila harder than if he'd been sympathetic.

'Don't be too hard on him, please. Not today.'

'I won't. I'm not a complete idiot.'

'Thanks.' That was all she had the right to ask. 'Nothing about my leaving early is his fault. It's me.'

'Fair enough.' He nodded. 'We'd better get you downstairs.'

The sooner she left Cornwall, the better it'd be for everyone.

An hour later, she settled into her seat on the coach and wedged herself in by the window. They started the slow drive up through Cornwall, and Lila peered in vain out through the steamed-up glass. On a nice morning it'd be a pleasant drive, but with today's thick rain they could be anywhere on the face of the planet. The friendly middle-aged lady sitting next to her tried to strike up a conversation and was clearly unimpressed by Lila's lack of response. The knowledge that they still had more than six hours to go darkened Lila's mood.

She lay back against the head rest and closed her eyes. If nothing else, that might quieten her travelling companion without the need for Lila to be blatantly rude.

You thought. That's the last thing you did.

Grant's words had haunted her all night while she tried in vain to sleep, and again when she paced around her room in the early hours of the morning. He was wrong. She *had* thought. Over and over again. She'd argued in her head the pros and cons of breaking a promise to her friend, and hadn't taken the decision to remain silent lightly. When Marlene Cross phoned Lila three years ago today and woke her from a deep sleep, she'd known it would be bad news.

Marlene, Belle's best friend from her schooldays and the matron of honour at her wedding, had taken on the painful task of calling a long list of Belle's friends to ease the Warrens' burden.

Lila's horror had brought her within a hair's breadth of blurting out that she'd been afraid this might happen, but somehow she'd allowed the moment to pass. Having lied by omission once, it became harder to admit the truth until she buried it deep enough to almost forget, but only almost. She'd lived with her guilt until she met Grant, and then everything changed. Before, it'd always been her boyfriends stretching the truth and letting her down; but with Grant, she'd been the deceitful one from the beginning. Gripped by the power of her instant attraction to him, it'd blinded her to the awful fact that she'd been instrumental in causing him the worst kind of pain.

'We're coming into Plymouth now. I do love a good day out shopping here,' the woman tried again, and Lila opened her eyes. She'd consider being friendly to her unwanted companion another penance and suck it up.

'Really? Do tell me about it,' Lila responded with a bright smile.

'Oh, you're American. How lovely. I went to Florida once . . . '

★　★　★

Grant shivered and pulled his long black woollen coat around himself. Turning up the collar did nothing to ward off the frigid wind whipping in off the sea or the lashing rain stinging his face. He surveyed the growing crowd, all laughing and joking around despite the terrible weather as they stripped down to swimsuits or fancy-dress costumes. Wetsuits were considered a cop-out, and anyone wearing them would be roundly mocked. The first year they were married, he'd allowed Belle to talk him into joining her, and afterwards he'd sworn never to do it again. He'd hike for miles across the moors without complaint and get wet and muddy, but her compulsion to plunge into icy waters bewildered him.

He recognised a small group of women running across the wet sand and inched his way forward to see them better. He shoved his hands deep into his pockets as the five remaining 'Belle's Belles' headed towards the sea. With their gold bikinis and gold high heels, topped off by cheap sparkling tiaras in their hair, they stood out from the crowd. Their costumes made complete sense to anyone who'd known Belle, because she'd started the group and never been one for blending in. After the swim, he knew they'd all go to Jack's Kitchen on the harbour and eat a huge cooked breakfast, washed down with gallons of sweet, hot tea.

A booming voice rang out over the loudspeakers. 'Time to freeze off the turkey and Christmas pudding you stuffed yourselves with yesterday so you can go home and eat the leftovers. Get ready for the fifty-second annual

Port Carne Polar Bear Plunge.'

Before he could consider using any common sense, Grant ripped off his coat and shucked off his thick jumper and sweatpants, leaving him in only his boxers and sports shorts. He took off running.

'Five. Four. Three. Two. One. Go.'

The first splash of icy water sucked the breath from his lungs but he kept going, plunging into the crashing waves. An exhilarating rush soared through him, and the sensation of being truly alive for the first time in years lit up his body.

'Join us!' Marlene yelled over at him. 'We're going to do Belle's Challenge.'

He took hold of her outstretched hand. Belle's competitive streak meant she'd always wanted to stay in longer and swim out further than anyone else. Her group did the ritual together and performed a taunting victory dance in the waves when they succeeded.

'Here we go!' Marlene shouted.

'Is this where — '

She glared. 'Don't. We honour her best *this* way, not by rehashing what we can't change.'

Grant nodded and didn't say another word. He'd heard far too much about that awful day. Belle's collapse in the waves. The women dragging her back to the beach. The local doctor's fruitless efforts to perform CPR. He pushed it all away and forced his attention back to the moment. They passed every one of the other swimmers before turning around and waving their hands in the air while jumping up and down like crazed lunatics.

'Race you all to the beach,' Marlene ordered, and everyone plunged back into the water.

Stepping out onto the sand, Grant shuddered as a blast of cold rainy air hit him full on, turning his skin into a shivering purple mass of goose pimples.

'Didn't you bring a towel?' Marlene asked, completely covered in a voluminous hooded bright pink robe.

His teeth chattered so violently he

could barely shake his head.

'Here's a spare.' She tossed him a large red towel and he quickly wrapped it around himself. 'I didn't plan to do this,' he admitted.

'She'd be pleased.' Marlene pointed over to a bright green case fixed on the sea wall. 'Did you see what we bought for her?'

Grant stared at the box.

'It's an automated external defibrillator. The beauty of this is anyone can use it with or without training.'

'This could've saved Belle,' his voice cracked out.

'Maybe. Maybe not. But it wasn't here.' Marlene's brisk response took him aback. 'She made her own choice and wasn't a believer in 'what ifs', was she?'

Grant reluctantly agreed.

'You're shivering, and so are we. Come and join us for breakfast.'

'Thanks, but maybe another day. Could I ring you up for a chat sometime?'

169

Marlene smiled. 'Of course. Go and have a long, hot shower before you come down with pneumonia. You're not Belle's Belles tough.' She struck a dramatic bodybuilder pose and he couldn't help laughing. 'I'm off.' She disappeared to join the rest of the group.

All of a sudden, Grant noticed a small brass plaque on the wall and crossed the cold, wet sand to get close enough to read the words.

Given in celebration of the vibrant life of Belle Warren Hawkins by Belle's Belles, Polar Bear Plunge swimmers extraordinary!

His vision blurred. He could blame the rain, but more likely it was due to the emotions roiling through him. This morning had given him a lot of thinking to do. He couldn't get the word choice out of his head. Lila said the same to him on the cliff when he'd questioned her determination to climb down to rescue the stranded boy.

Grant trudged back to where he'd

abandoned his clothes. He struggled to pull them back on, as everything stuck to his damp skin. After dragging his coat on, he started to make his way off the beach and back to the harbour. He garnered a few curious stares from people who recognised him but didn't stop to speak to any of them. Then he dragged up the hill up to Mendelby House, but hesitated outside the front gate. If Belle's parents spotted him, it'd mean too many difficult explanations, and they'd get upset. He'd creep in around the back and hopefully make it to the cottage without being spotted.

'Where on earth have you been?'

Grant froze with his hand on the doorknob and turned to face Nick.

'I don't believe it.' His angry gaze swept down over Grant. 'How could you?'

16

'Come inside. I need to warm up,' Grant explained without stopping to give Nick a proper reply. 'Stick the kettle on while I go and take a shower.'

'But . . .'

'Nick, I'll talk all you want after I stop myself from getting hypothermia.' The insidious cold reached deep into his bones, and he understood the Belles' insistence on immediate greasy food and hot drinks. He retreated to the bathroom, and after the hottest shower he could stand, dragged on layers of warm clothes: thick fleecy sweatpants, a black polo neck, a chunky Aran jumper and woollen socks. He couldn't wear anything else and still be able to walk. He dried his hair and struggled to drag a comb through the tangled up curls. Tomorrow he'd make getting it cut a priority. He ran a hand over his unshaven jaw, but decided to leave it alone for now, and strode back to the kitchen. 'Right. That's better.'

'Have you eaten?' Nick asked.

'No. Are you offering to cook?' Grant's teasing question brought a weak smile to his friend's face. They both knew that Nick's acquaintance with kitchens came purely through eating in them. Grant hacked off a couple of thick slices of Edith's homemade wheat bread and popped them into the toaster. 'That should hold body and soul together for a while.'

'I did make the tea.'

'Well done. Pour me a mug.'

They didn't talk while Grant got his breakfast ready. He carried his plate over to over the sofa and flopped down. 'God, that feels good. I'm worn out. It's been too much for my old legs these last few days.'

Nick settled into the armchair by the window. 'So, do I get an explanation?'

'Have you ever done the swim?'

'Yeah, once when I was young and

stupid. But you're avoiding the question. We're not talking about me.'

Grant took a mouthful of tea and wondered how best to answer. He'd already made the decision not to mention Lila and the emails. 'I needed to at least try to understand why Belle did the swim even though she'd been having some heart issues.' A fresh wave of despair swept through him. 'Why would she risk everything we had for a few minutes of lunacy?'

'Because that was Belle,' Nick muttered, 'and it's the way she was. You *know* that. My sister thought she was invincible.'

'I'm sorry. I really didn't mean to stir everything back up.'

'Did it help you?'

'Yes, oddly enough it did.' Haltingly he began to run through the whole episode, and couldn't keep from smiling when he recounted his appearance as one of Belle's Belles.

'Did they stick you in a gold bikini?' Nick gibed.

'Good Lord, no.'

'Be very grateful. Belle would've done it in a second.'

'She certainly would if she'd tracked down one to fit me.'

'Did you see the memorial they did for her?'

'Yes. It sort of shocked me. I'd no idea. Why did no one tell me about it?'

'Marlene promised me that she did at the time.' Nick frowned. 'You sure you didn't blow her off? You haven't been very communicative.'

Vague memories of the huge number of phone messages, emails and letters he'd received and either deleted or thrown in the bin flooded back to Grant. He'd been unable to deal with people's clumsy attempts at sympathy and coped by simply ignoring them. *Just like my father.*

'If I hadn't turned up on your door-step at regular intervals you would've blanked me out too.'

The blunt statement of fact sliced right through Grant. 'You're right.'

'Halleluiah! At last we're getting

somewhere,' Nick cheered. Instantly his smile disappeared. 'If we're on a roll here, go ahead and tell me what you did to run Lila off.'

'Run her off? What're you talking about?'

'She's gone back to London. Went on the coach this morning. Didn't you know?'

Grant shook his head. Now what had he done?

* * *

Lila yawned and wondered what to do with the long day ahead. She'd barely managed a wink of sleep last night in the bland hotel suite and couldn't stop wishing herself back in Edith Warren's cramped attic bedroom. She missed the swaths of pink rose wallpaper, the tiny single bed decked out in white lace, and the small lead-paned window overlooking the garden. Most of all, she missed Grant. His unrestrained laughter when she cracked a joke. The way he tilted his head slightly when he really listened to something. And most of all his achingly gentle touch, redolent with so much promise. *You'd better get used to being without it all, because last night he made it perfectly clear what he thought of you.*

Until now, she'd focused on her career and not been overly bothered when relationships didn't work out; but in a few short days, Grant had turned all of that upside down and left her reeling. If she didn't do something to take her mind off the whole mess, she'd go mad. There wasn't any actual meeting today, but she could still tinker with the new display images she'd created. She was in charge of L'Oiseau's overall concept, but took ideas from the various countries and adjusted the plans to suit the different customer bases.

Lila settled in a cosy chair with her laptop and opened the file she'd been working on. Twenty unproductive minutes later, she gave up and slammed the lid in disgust. She gazed out of the window, and the persistent drizzle smudged the scene in front of her, giving it the blurred look of an Impressionist painting. A bright flash of red from a little girl's umbrella as she danced along the street caught her eye. Maybe a good long walk would exorcise her demons. Lila's phone buzzed with an incoming text message, but she ignored it and hurried off to find her trainers.

Back home she often walked in downtown Nashville on her lunch break, favouring either Centennial Park or the riverfront depending on her mood. At weekends she frequently went hiking with friends or indulged in one of her favourite high-risk pursuits like bouldering or hang-gliding.

But you design shop window displays to sell make-up.

Grant had disappointed her by making the same mistake as a lot of other men and equating her ultra-feminine appearance with physical weakness. Luckily he had redeemed himself by apologising and asking her to forgive him.

I'd forgive you anything, but you couldn't do the same for me.

Thank goodness she'd found out now before he completely broke her heart instead of simply chipping away a multitude of tiny cracks. In two short weeks she'd be gone from London to start on a whirlwind tour of Europe to oversee the new displays. Afterwards she'd return to Nashville, write a polite thank-you note to the Warrens, and put all this behind her.

Lila grabbed her room key card before leaving, and outside the hotel took off at a brisk place. Somehow after a while she arrived back at the main door of the hotel with no clue how far she'd walked or where she'd been. She'd gone out wearing only a thin jacket over her jeans and jumper and was now soaking wet and freezing. Grant would say she obviously wasn't English because they were all born with an umbrella in one hand and wearing a raincoat.

Get out of my head, you frustrating man.

179

She stripped off and abandoned her soggy clothes in a heap on the floor before jumping into a scalding hot shower. After taking her time washing her hair and lathering it with conditioner, she got out to dry off. Lila slathered on the new elderflower cream from the L'Oiseau skin treatment line, but as it scented the air she almost jumped back in the shower to wash it off. Yesterday Grant told her how wonderful she smelled.

She rifled through her meagre wardrobe, rejected her Christmas jumpers and settled on a black and white checked blouse and black corduroy trousers. Lila's stomach rumbled, but she couldn't face dining alone in the hotel's supposedly excellent restaurant. She'd hardly eaten at all yesterday after skipping breakfast and only buying a cup of coffee and a stale pastry at one of the motorway service stations when the coach made a stop to pick up more passengers.

Lila opened the mini-fridge and selected a bottle of orange juice and a bag of peanuts. That would do for now. She drank the juice straight down to quench her thirst and started on the nuts. Her phone buzzed, and when she saw Grant's number appear on the screen she turned the volume to silent. Lila scrolled down through to check what other messages she'd missed. One from Nick. Another from Edith. The other twenty or so were all from Grant. The first few said that he needed to talk to her and asked her to ring him back. Lila read the next batch and noticed the change in his tone. These were more despondent, and stated that he understood why she was ignoring him and blamed himself for being difficult. The last message simply asked her to give him a chance to explain his thoughts and feelings.

What for? There was no point. They could talk from now until next Christmas and never get past the brick wall of Belle's untimely death. If Lila didn't feel so unbearably sad, she'd laugh out loud at the notion of Grant wanting to explain his thoughts and feelings. He'd been around her too long.

She pressed her finger firmly on the delete button and erased all his messages, then scanned over Nick's brief text.

Click on this link. You'll be surprised.

Lila couldn't resist, and as the newspaper picture filled the screen her mouth gaped open in shock.

17

Grant froze outside Lila's door. He'd walked up the five flights of stairs instead of taking the lift to give himself more time to calm down, but it hadn't done a thing for his nerves. If it hadn't been for Nick reining him in, he would've left Cornwall on the coach late yesterday and arrived in London this morning around six — an even worse idea than waiting for the trains to run again and turning up this afternoon.

'Excuse me, sir — are you . . . going in?'

He jerked around to stare at the uniformed waiter pushing a loaded room-service cart, and plainly wondering what Grant was up to.

'Yes. I'm visiting Miss Caswell.'

The man nodded and gestured towards the door as if to say, 'Follow through, then. I'm watching you.' At Grant's first knock, the door flew open and he stared at Lila. Her stark black and white outfit emphasised the shadows under her tired eyes but couldn't dim her innate loveliness.

'Good. That was quick — I'm starving.' A rush of heat coloured Lila's pale cheeks as she registered his presence. 'Grant! What on earth are you doing here?' She glanced behind him. 'Sorry, I didn't see you there for a moment. Bring it on in, please.'

'Certainly, madam.' The waiter wheeled the cart around Grant and disappeared inside the room.

'I'm sorry. I'm disturbing your meal.'

'It's not a problem.' Lila's gaze bored into him. 'Do I get an answer to my question?'

'I think you need to . . . ' Grant nodded towards the man hovering around.

'Oh, yeah.' She fumbled in her pocket and pulled out some money to give the man a tip. 'I suppose you'd better come in.'

It wasn't the most gracious invitation, but at least she hadn't thrown him out on his ear. Yet.

'Do you like hamburgers?'

Grant frowned.

'Even for you, it shouldn't be a hard question. Yes or no?'

'Um, yes, but why are you asking?' He received the weary look of a teacher dealing with an inattentive pupil.

'They've brought me hamburgers and fries. That was my way of asking if you'd care to join me.'

Grant shifted from one foot to the other. 'Don't feel you need to be polite. There won't be enough for us both.'

Lila sighed. 'I ordered too much and their portions are generous. For heaven's sake, don't turn this into a big deal.'

'Sorry.' He always seemed to be apologising to her, either in person or in his head.

'Help yourself to a drink.' She gestured towards the mini-fridge. 'I ordered myself a Coke with extra ice, but I'm not sharing.'

If he'd blinked, Grant would've missed her brief smile. A sliver of hope trickled into his bloodstream. He grabbed a bottle of water and sat down before he could make any more dumb comments.

'We'll talk after we've eaten. I'm starving and haven't had anything all day.'

'Me neither.' Discovering she'd left Cornwall because of him had killed Grant's appetite. It made no difference what explanation she'd given the Warrens about her reasons for leaving; he knew the truth.

Neither of them spoke until they'd eaten their way down to the last crumb. 'That's better.' Lila leaned back in the chair and rested her hands on her stomach. 'For an English hamburger, that wasn't too bad.'

'Anything's good when you're hungry.'

'Gotta disagree with you there. Black pudding? Yuck.'

'Heathen. You don't appreciate decent food,' he played along with her.

'If you ever come to Nashville, I'll try you on chitlins and see if you're of the same opinion.' Her voice wavered. 'They're the small intestines of a pig and very much an acquired taste.'

'I might take your word for that.'

'You mean you wouldn't consider trying them, or that the idea of travelling to Nashville is completely outside . . . '

Grant shrugged. There was so much to say, and he'd no idea where to start.

'How about we begin by swapping our 'getting wet' stories? I got soaked taking a walk this morning, but I wasn't as wet as you apparently managed to get.' Lila found the picture and shoved her phone across the table. 'Blame Nick.'

Conflicting emotions flitted across his face, and his heavy sigh betrayed the fact he'd rather not discuss his bizarre decision to do the Polar Bear Plunge. *Tough.* Belle might have let him get away with it, but she wasn't Belle.

'That was brave of you.'

'Not really.' He stared at her. 'It wasn't planned, and I certainly didn't intend to be in the local paper today.'

'I bet the Warrens' phone is ringing off the hook. That journalist will be desperate for an interview now.'

'Not going to happen,' he scoffed.

Lila held her tongue. If she waited long enough, he'd talk. For a largely Type A personality, she could be remarkably patient.

'I suppose you might as well hear the whole thing.' Anyone would think she'd spread-eagled him on a torture rack and was all set to turn the screws. Haltingly, he explained his urge to go to the beach and watch the traditional Boxing Day swim.

She bit back tears while trying to imagine him alone in a crowd of people, standing on the spot where he lost his beloved wife. He'd done it in a desperate effort to understand why Belle loved the occasion so much and the vivid pictures he drew with his words kept her spellbound.

'You'd love the Belles. They're your kind of women. Brave and fearless.' A faint smile softened Grant's stern expression and he quietly carried on. By the time he reached the part about the defibrillator, tears ran unabated down her face. Leaning across the table, he gently brushed them away. 'Marlene told me off when I railed against the unfairness of it all. She told me Belle wasn't a believer in what ifs, and she was right. She also told me it'd been Belle's choice.'

That didn't salve Lila's conscience one little bit.

'I'm still struggling with those emails,' he admitted. 'I shouldn't be, but I am.'

She couldn't blame him, no matter how desperately she wished it could be different. 'I could keep saying sorry from now until I'm old and grey, but I can't change what happened.'

Grant grasped her hands. 'I'm feeling better these days than I have done in three years. That's partly your doing.'

'I'm not sure what I've . . . '

'You, the Warrens, and Cornwall. The

trio of miracle workers. Something about the combination is working its magic on me.' A diffident smile crept across his face. 'I even rang my father on Christmas Day and we had a halfway friendly conversation.'

'That's amazing. I'm proud of you.'

'Thanks.' Grant told her briefly about his father's illness and shook his head. 'He must really be concerned or he wouldn't have shared any of that with me.'

Lila worded her response carefully. 'Have you considered going to see him?'

'Yes, but I'll wait until he gets the test results and then make up my mind.'

She considered suggesting that his father might be scared and need someone to help him through this, but held back. 'Good plan.' Relief warmed his eyes, and she guessed he'd expected her to push harder.

'Would you be willing to consider coming back to Cornwall for the New Year now we're, um . . . '

'Friends again?' Lila completed the

sentence for him.

'Yes, friends again. That is, if you haven't got too much work to do here?' The sparkle in his deep green eyes belied the supposedly serious question.

'I don't usually lie all the time,' Lila protested.

'The little white variety, done out of kindness, isn't a capital offence.'

'Maybe not.'

'So do I get an answer?'

'I'd love to.' A trickle of uncertainty settled in the base of her stomach. 'Maybe they won't want me.'

'Trust me, that won't be an issue,' Grant insisted. 'I'll authorise you to tell one more white lie and say your meetings finished early. It's the truth to say no one in your office is working again until after the New Year. Edith will no doubt kill yet another fatted calf, or at least a few more mince pies.'

'How can I possibly resist?'

'I really hope you can't.'

His earnest response ignited a surge of hope in Lila. 'Really?'

Grant pressed a soft kiss on her mouth. 'Yes, really.' He eased back and Lila knew she wasn't imagining the hint of regret behind his smile. 'I'd better go. I'm staying at my house in Watford tonight and getting the train back to Cornwall in the morning.'

They both stood up and slowly headed towards the door.

'Would you like a travelling companion?' she blurted out.

'I certainly would.' Grant kissed her cheek, sending a waft of his familiar cologne to arouse her senses. 'Please tell me it isn't too late to say Happy Christmas?'

'Never.'

'Good. The train leaves Paddington shortly after ten and even if traffic's bad it should only be about a ten-minute taxi ride from here.'

'Why don't you come over so we can go together? You could have breakfast with me downstairs first. Around eight thirty?'

'I'll be here.' Grant hesitated with his

hand on the lock. 'Thank you.'

'What for?'

'Listening and understanding. You don't know how much it means to me.'

Lila couldn't resist brushing away a stray dark curl from his forehead. 'One day you'll tell me. You're getting good at the whole communication thing.'

'Careful, now. Remember I'm a typical stubborn man.'

I could never forget that. It's one reason we've got ourselves in a tangled mess. That and my stupidity. 'I'll see you in the morning.' She couldn't let him leave without making her own apology. 'Thank you too for not writing me off.'

'I couldn't. I tried. But I couldn't.' With that simple statement and a wry smile, he left.

Lila closed the door and locked it behind him. Leaning back, she wrapped her arms around herself, unable to stop smiling. Simply knowing that Grant hadn't been able to stay away changed everything. Roll on tomorrow.

18

'Wow, you do clean up well.'

Grant flushed under Lila's frank, appreciative stare. He'd found a barber open late last night and indulged in a much-needed haircut and straight shave. Back home, he wielded the iron on a couple of shirts and packed clean clothes to take to Cornwall. He'd experienced a brief pang of guilt that morning when he teamed a pair of dark green jeans with a soft green and black checked shirt. It'd been the last outfit Belle put together for him, done because she always despaired of his non-existent fashion sense.

'Sorry, was that too personal?' Lila slapped her hand over her mouth.

'Only in a good way,' he reassured her. 'You're not looking too shabby yourself.'

'You flatterer.'

Hardly. If I was really trying to

impress, I'd tell you that suede jacket picks up the gold flecks in your eyes and the cream jumper makes your beautiful skin even more luminous. Grant said none of that, but a rush of heat flooded her face and he guessed she'd read his mind.

'Breakfast I think.' Her brisk manner amused him. 'I'm starving again.'

'Probably because a hamburger thief stole half of your dinner last night.'

'That must be it. In that case he owes me.'

Grant linked his arm with hers. 'He'd be honoured.'

'I should think so too,' Lila retorted. 'Oh, by the way, I called Edith last night and grovelled.' She threw him a questioning look. 'She didn't seem surprised to hear from me.'

'Fancy that.'

'Yeah, I did wonder if a little bird whispered in her ear.'

He kept his reaction to a shrug.

'Back to your tight-lipped self today, I see.' She poked him in the ribs and laughed when he jumped out of the way. 'Let's get a table. We'll call a truce while we eat.'

Doubtless she'd save the rest of her questions for the train, where he'd be a helpless captive for four and a half hours.

★   ★   ★

With the Tamar Bridge in sight and only another hour or so before they'd need to be getting ready, Grant seized his chance. Lila could give MI6 a run for their money. He'd watched her mentally cataloguing his confessions, from his insistence on always using loose tea instead of tea bags to his fanatical recycling habits, and the fact he never missed an episode of *Corona- tion Street*.

I'd always wriggle up on my mum's lap and we'd watch it together. She'd drink an enormous mug of tea and I'd have a glass of orange squash. We had a biscuit tin open next to us and she never counted how many I ate. She'd talk to me about the characters as if they were old friends.

After they'd lost her, his father attempted to stop Grant from watching the programme, but he'd stood up for himself and kicked up such a fuss that Ian finally gave in.

It kept you close to her when he'd taken everything else away. Lila was spot on as usual.

'Is it my turn now?'

'For what?' She stared at him, obviously confused.

'To turn the tables on you.'

Lila grimaced. 'I guess.'

'You'd rather have wisdom teeth pulled out without any anaesthetic?'

'Of course not. I'm an open book.'

Anyone who said that was usually the complete opposite, and gradually he winkled out Lila's life story, her likes and dislikes. 'You hate ice cream? Seriously? *No one* hates ice cream.'

'Well, I do.' The forceful declaration made him laugh. 'It's not funny.'

'Oh, but it is. I thought Americans ate more ice cream than anyone else.'

'Depends which survey you read. Some say it's Australia or New Zealand.'

'That still doesn't explain *you*,' he teased.

'It's too . . . cold and slimy and . . . '

Grant roared — he couldn't help it, wiping away tears as she glared at him; and the other people in their carriage threw them strange looks.

'I didn't make fun of your quirks,' Lila protested.

'Ah, but there are quirks and quirks and yours easily top mine.' He'd better shut up before she got mad. 'Tell me about your job.'

'Wise man.' She wagged her finger at him. 'I drifted into it really. My degree is in interior design but I couldn't get a job straight after graduation and got an offer of temporary work in L'Oiseau as a sales clerk. One day the window designer didn't turn up, and my boss told me to put something together. It kind of mushroomed from there.'

'You travel a lot?'

Lila nodded. 'Yes. We're an international company and I've been all over the world.' She rushed on, disliking the hint of defensiveness entering her voice. 'And before you ask, I've never been averse to the idea of marriage or children, but it hasn't happened and I'm good with that.'

'You've given up the idea?'

They were supposed to be truthful to each other. 'I wouldn't say that,' Lila grudgingly replied.

Grant rested his elbows on the table and she couldn't avoid his penetrating gaze. 'Then what *would* you say?' His whispered question sent a shiver running right through her.

'I'd say I've got an open mind. I'm not out there searching, but if the right man comes along, who knows?' She stumbled over her words.

'That's all I need.' He relaxed back in the seat with a satisfied smile.

Thanks for putting me through that.

'Good, because it's all you're getting.'

'We're nearly there. The next station is ours, and Nick should be waiting.'

'You never did tell me what's up with him.'

Grant checked his watch. 'There isn't time for the whole story now. Come up to the cottage after supper and we'll talk.'

'That's a — '

'Go on. Say the word. It won't bite either of us.'

'Are you sure?'

'Absolutely.'

'Okay.' She took a deep breath. 'That's a date.'

'Perfect.' Grant jumped up. 'Time to move.' He made short work of getting their luggage out by the door and then leaned back against the carriage wall, focusing on the scenery flying by outside the open window. Lila loved the way the wind messed up his newly short curls. She actually preferred his old rumpled look, but kept that to herself. She guessed this was all part of his effort to get to a new version of normal.

The train came to a noisy, grinding halt, and out on the platform Nick hugged her and shook hands with Grant.

'I didn't expect you two back here together anytime soon.' His wry comment, accompanied by a lot of eye-rolling, said that was exactly what he had predicted.

'Like to keep you guessing, mate.' Grant's flippant reply earned him a punch in the arm from Nick, and they scrapped like a couple of schoolboys. Lila stood to one side until they finally stopped.

'I'll drop you off at the house and see you properly later,' Nick explained. 'I've got to go and help Dad in the shop until closing time.'

Grant frowned. 'Is he all right?'

'Bit tired, I think.'

Lila picked up on something unsaid between the two men but didn't interfere. On the short drive, they kept the conversation light, talking about how crowded London was and the fact they were both relieved to be back in Cornwall.

Nick stopped the car outside the front gate. 'There you go. Tell Mum I'll make sure we're back by six for our pasties. Dad will try to stay late after being closed for Christmas, but I won't let him.'

Grant insisted on carrying her bags as well as his own, and they made their way up the narrow path. Before they reached the front door, Lila felt his gaze on her. 'I'm really pleased you came back,' he said. 'I didn't expect to get a second chance.'

'Neither did I.'

'It's the first time I've looked forward to the New Year in . . . ages.'

They both knew he'd been about to say three years, but she didn't prompt him to spell it out.

Edith appeared in the doorway, beaming at them both. 'Come in, my dears. I heard our Nick's car. I bet he sneaked off back to the shop. John will appreciate the help, although he won't admit it.' Her smile faded a touch before resurfacing even brighter. 'I've got the kettle boiling and I made more mince pies this morning.'

'Lead me to them,' Lila declared, giving up on the idea of getting back into her tighter jeans this side of the holidays.

The rest of the day slipped away, and finally Grant gave her a sly wink across the room. 'I'm going to call it a day.' He stood up and stretched, giving a big yawn. 'Lila, your laptop is still in my backpack. I'll go out to the cottage and bring it in, unless you want to wait until the morning.'

'I really need it tonight. I'll walk out with you.' Lila could've smacked him when he started to protest. *Don't make this hard work.* 'I could do with the fresh air and you're tired.' *Give in now, or else.*

'Well, all right.'

Don't sound quite so reluctant.

The minute they stepped outside the

back door, Grant reached for her hand and she tightened her fingers around his. They idled their way down through the garden and along the slightly overgrown path to the cottage.

'Were you impressed by my acting?' he said.

'You were terrible. Please stick to carpentry. You don't know when to quit,' Lila joked, and he pulled her into his arms.

'Oh yes I do.' Grant smiled, the shadows dancing across his face in the moonlight. 'And it's not yet.'

'You'd better hurry up and tell me what's going on with Nick and his father before someone comes looking for me. They'll think I've lost my way back to the house if I take too long.'

He warmed her with a long, searching stare. 'I don't know about you, but I think I've finally found my way after straying from the path for a very long time.'

A new lightness unravelled inside of Lila, and she smiled.

'Come on in and give me the wisdom of your feminine intuition.'

'Said the spider to the fly,' Lila teased, and allowed him to lead her inside.

19

'Tell me more about the shop.'

Lila's question took Grant by surprise. 'The shop? I thought you'd be more interested in Nick's job offer.' He'd already run through the small amount of information Nick had told him, and she'd listened in silence.

'Yeah, but we're on the same page there. I totally agree with you. Of course he must seize the opportunity. He'll end up being resentful if he turns it down, and that's not good for him or anyone else.'

'But it's not that simple,' Grant protested.

Lila's satisfied expression told him he was wrong, and she'd prove it. 'If you know what you're aiming for, the rest is detail.' She shifted from the sofa to perch on the arm of his chair with her loose silky hair brushing against his shoulder. 'I know you think I'm crazy, but go along with me for a minute.'

'Okay. I give in.' *I always do around you.* 'Warren's Hardware has been a fixture in the village for nearly a hundred years. John took over from his father, and it's a simple old-fashioned hardware shop. I'm sure you have the same kind of places selling nails, wood, paint, mouse traps, anything you need really.' He shrugged. 'They've struggled to keep their heads above water for the last ten years or so because of competition from the big out-of-town shops. The holiday visitors don't often need what John sells either, so it's an uphill battle.'

She paced around the small room before turning to face him again. 'I want you to take me to see the shop tomorrow.'

'Are you planning to wave your magic window-display wand? Even you would have a hard time making tins of paint look appealing.'

'Oh ye of little faith,' Lila joked. 'I've

got a few ideas, but until I see the shop they might all be ridiculous.' She gave him a long stare. 'Do you enjoy living in London?'

'Do I what?'

'You heard me.'

The school teacher edge to her voice made him smile, but only inwardly, because he wasn't a complete idiot. 'I don't know what that's got to do with Nick and the shop, but to keep you happy and off my back I don't mind admitting I don't care much for it these days.'

'I thought not.'

'What's going through your devious brain now?'

'Oh, nothing much. It's a wild idea.' Her hazel eyes sparkled. 'I'll share it with you when the moment's right.'

Grant stood and held out his hands, gently pulling her up into his arms. 'You're a challenging woman.'

'Boring wouldn't interest you, would it?'

He shook his head. 'We'll do the tour

tomorrow morning, and you can amaze me with your brilliance.' Privately he couldn't envision a way to solve the problem and keep everyone happy, but if it kept her smiling at him he'd walk over hot coals.

'Thanks.' Lila popped a light kiss on his mouth. 'You're a star.'

No, you are. You came sparkling into my life and sprinkled fairy dust over my gloomy existence. 'I can't imagine going back to 'normal' next week.'

'If it's any consolation, I can't imagine it either.'

Her needle-sharp response stunned him. Grant cleared his throat, struggling to say something; anything that didn't come across as totally out of line.

Lila touched a finger to his lips. 'Wait. Not now. I'll see you in the morning.'

'Sleep well.'

'You too.'

'Don't forget your laptop.'

She burst into girlish giggles. 'That would sure raise a few eyebrows, wouldn't it?' Lila headed for the sofa to pick it up but stopped by the coffee table. Her hand hovered over the small silver-framed photograph of Belle, the one he always took with him when he travelled. 'Do you think she'd mind?'

Grant didn't need to ask what she meant. 'I hope not. I don't think so. Do you?'

Lila firmly shook her head. 'She loved us both.' Without saying anything else, she walked over to the door. 'Good night. Again.'

He walked outside with her and leaned against the wall where he could watch her make her way back down the path. *Is she right, Belle? I hope so. I can't bear the idea of hurting you, but I need this.* Not until the last star disappeared from the sky did he go back into the cottage and lock the door for the night.

* * *

Lila's heart did a little flip as Grant strolled into the kitchen, his hair still

210

damp from the shower, and back to his normal ragged jeans and a thick dark green jumper. She focused on her scrambled eggs to avoid gawking like a teenage girl with her first crush.

'What's everyone doing today?' Edith asked.

Grant poured himself a large mug of tea and popped two slices of thick bread into the toaster. 'Lila wants to experience the delights of Port Carne in the winter, complete with closed-up shops and a bitter wind blowing in off the sea. If she's lucky, it'll decide to rain as well.' He laughed and grabbed his toast before pulling out the chair next to her to sit down. 'Can you believe she hasn't been in your shop yet? She wasted her time last week looking at sticks of rock and rude postcards instead of screwdrivers and wallpaper.' He slathered a thick layer of butter on his toast and reached for Edith's homemade blackberry jam. 'Funny girl.'

His indulgent smile made Lila blush,

and she shovelled a forkful of eggs into her mouth.

'You're a naughty boy,' Edith half-heartedly told him off. 'You'll enjoy it, dear.' She nodded at Lila. 'A bit of fresh air never hurt no one.'

'You don't need to worry about lunch for us. We'll get something out.'

We will? he thought.

'Isn't he a sweetheart?' Her pithy comment made Grant colour up this time, so at least they were equal on the embarrassment front.

'John and Nick went down early today. We always have a January sale, and my poor man's fretting over getting things ready,' Edith explained.

'Are there enough people around this time of year to make it worthwhile?' Lila asked before stopping to wonder if she'd sounded rude. 'I didn't mean . . . '

Edith patted her hand. 'Don't fret, love. You're right. He'll only sell a few half-price tins of paint, but his father and grandfather always held a sale then, and another in July, so that's what my John does. He's a creature of habit and I've given up trying to change him.'

Someone needs to, or he'll either keel over from working too hard or go bankrupt. 'My father's equally stubborn.' Lila steered the conversation away from John Warren, and the good humour return to Edith's strained expression. 'That's men for you.'

'Ahem.' Grant cleared his throat. 'Anyone remembered I'm here?'

As if I could forget you. 'I need to go and finish getting ready,' Lila said, 'and I'll be back down here in ten minutes ready to go.'

He bent down close her ear, and she was relieved to see Edith busy at the sink washing dishes. 'Skip the make-up today. You're on holiday. No one's going to tell on you to your fancy firm.'

'It's nothing to do with where I do or don't work.' The mischievous glint in Grant's eyes told her he recognised another lie when he heard one. 'Fine. Am I allowed perfume, or is that banned too?'

'Oh, you're allowed that,' Grant murmured. 'The flowery one you wore yesterday would be my choice.'

Her face flamed.

'I'll get my jacket and meet you in the hall.' He gave her a wink and hurried from the room.

Edith glanced over her shoulder. 'It's good to hear the boy laugh again.'

All of a sudden, the awkwardness of the situation swamped Lila, and tears pricked at her eyes.

'Don't you dare get maudlin on me,' Edith warned. 'My Belle loved that man more than anything, but she'd hate him to be lonely the rest of his life. She didn't pick her best friends lightly, either.'

'I know.' Lila's raspy voice betrayed her battle to stay in control. 'I never expected . . . ' She flailed her hands in a gesture of confusion.

'Nor did he, I'm sure, my dear. We can't plan these things.' Edith chuckled. 'My mother had her eye on Phillip Walker for me because he worked for a solicitor up in St. Austell.' She rolled her eyes. 'But he were a stuck-up little so and so. I told them I'd have John and no one else.'

'But how did you know for sure?'

'If you have to ask me that question, then Grant's not the right one for you.'

The sage response brought Lila up short. She didn't really *need* to ask, because her heart knew the truth. 'Fair enough.' She jumped up. 'I'll be late in a minute.'

'He's right about something else too.' Edith smirked. 'You don't need any of that stuff on your face.'

Lila tilted her chin and left the room with as much dignity as she could muster.

20

Grant hated to rush Lila, but feared his feet might turn into blocks of ice if they stood outside Warren's Hardware much longer. They'd walked the nearby streets for the last hour while Lila made notes about the different shops and what they sold. She'd gone inside all the ones that were open and checked them out. Lila chatted non-stop to everyone they met, answered numerous questions about her accent, and generally ingratiated herself to the population of Port Carne. 'Are you ready to go in?'

'Yeah, we can now.' Lila smiled and linked her arm with his. 'You're a patient man. I hadn't realised quite how much until this morning. I suppose teachers need enormous reserves of patience, and carpentry isn't for anyone in a hurry either.'

'I suppose.' He pushed open the door

and the familiar smell of good hardware shops everywhere assailed his nostrils. The indefinable mix of turpentine, raw wood and sandpaper always soothed him. 'Hallo, John. I've brought Lila to see where you spend your days. Where's Nick?'

John stood behind the counter sorting loose screws into plastic boxes. 'He's gone out for coffee. My jar of instant isn't good enough for him. He prefers the fancy stuff at that pricey new café on Cliff Street.' The good-natured rant stopped and he eyed up Lila. 'What do you think of my little empire?'

Oh, God, don't ask her that. She'll probably tell you and you won't care for it one bit.

'It's pretty impressive. Edith said you're getting ready for a sale.' While she talked, Lila wandered around, picking up the occasional tool and scrutinising the displays.

'I suppose she said I'm wasting my time.'

Grant prayed she'd be tactful.

'I got the impression she's a little concerned, but she's got faith in you,' she said.

John nodded. 'Knowing my better half, she weren't that kind.'

'There aren't many places like this left where I live,' Lila commented. 'It's all what we call big-box stores. The personal touch is mostly gone.'

'That's the way of it.' John shook his head. 'This place will disappear the same way soon because I don't see my boy taking over. He didn't do all that accountant training to sell nuts and bolts, did he?'

Neither of them answered. If Grant passed that nugget of information on later, it might help Nick feel better about his decision.

'We'll let you get on with your work.'

'Grant's taking me out for lunch.' Lila beamed. 'Where do you recommend?'

'Don't listen to any suggestions he gives you.' Nick breezed back into the shop, bringing with him a blast of cold air. 'His idea of gourmet cuisine is eating a pasty with a knife and fork instead of out of the paper bag. Take her to the Lifeboat House, mate.'

'Overpriced, and . . .'

Nick cut his father off. 'The chef's top-notch. Someone bought the old lifeboat house when they built a new one, gutted it and turned it into a great restaurant. All locally sourced food, and it's not pretentious, no matter what he says.' He cocked a thumb in John's direction.

'He's only saying that because he's got his eye on the head waitress. Pretty girl with red hair. She's the attraction. That's why he's over there every five minutes.' John grinned.

'Well, I think it sounds neat.' Lila piped up and stopped the father/son argument mid-stream.

'The Lifeboat House it is.' Grant reached for her hand, tucking it into his own and ignoring the interested glances they received.

'See y'all later.' Lila's warm drawl always made him smile. He could listen to her all day.

'You want to walk down by the harbour first and then eat?' He sensed her brain bubbling with ideas and guessed it'd be better to get it out in the open now.

'Are you afraid I'll talk too much and spoil lunch?'

'Never.' His dry comment earned him a playful smack. 'Hey, what did I do to deserve that?'

'How about know me far too well after such a short time?'

'Is there such a thing as 'too well'?' Grant probed.

'Doesn't it bother you, even a little?'

'Bother? Not sure that's the right word.'

'Scare. Bewilder. Confuse. Any of those work instead?' she asked, cocking her head to one side.

Grant took hold of her hands, rubbing his fingers over the bruises and scratches still lingering from their

Christmas Eve rescue. 'I hope you don't think I'm rushing you into anything, because I don't mean to.'

'Then what *do* you mean?' The nervous tremor running through her voice warned him that he'd better get this right. She hadn't intended to put him on the spot, but the question popped out before she could censor her mouth. All thoughts of lunch or the hardware shop flew away, and her whole attention focused on the man standing in front of her. He pulled her into his arms and sighed when she rested her head on his broad, warm chest.

'I care for you, Lila. Very much. I get the feeling that if we spend more time together, we'll discover we want to explore something long-term.' His calm certainty eased her mind. 'Tell me if I'm way out of line and I'll back off now.' She met his steady emerald gaze. 'I won't like it, but . . . '

'Kiss me.' Lila's whispered request brought out another of Grant's dazzling smiles, the sort she couldn't resist and didn't even want to anymore. 'You're absolutely on the right track.'

'Thank goodness.' Immediately he followed her instructions to the letter. 'Better?' Grant asked when he finally stopped kissing her.

'Much.'

'Right. Now we've settled that, it's time you bombarded me with your bizarre ideas.'

'What makes you think they're not completely sensible?' Lila smiled as he raised his dark, straight eyebrows skywards. 'Let's sit on that empty bench.'

Grant glanced around. 'They're all empty. Who else would linger outside in this frigid weather?'

'It means we won't be overheard, doesn't it?' She strode off, settling herself down while he made his way over to join her. 'Leave Nick out of the equation for minute. We'll take it as a given that he won't be here.' Lila shushed Grant's attempt to protest. 'Also put to one side John's age and state of health. Focus solely on the shop and what can be done to improve turnover.' Briskly she ran through what she'd seen in the nearby shops. 'You don't want to completely get rid of the hardware side, because it'd be missed, but we'd streamline it down to the basics. I keep hearing a lot about all the second homes and rental cottages around here, and they all need decorating and continual maintenance. We could create a uniquely Cornish look to suit the environment; that would be our main focus.'

'We?' he interrupted. 'Don't get me wrong, because this all sounds amazing, but next week you'll be knee deep in your job again and I'll be back making kitchen cabinets in Watford.'

'What if we weren't?' Lila tossed out the idea and waited. The colour drained from Grant's face. A pair of squawking seagulls broke the silence and for once she was grateful to the ugly birds.

'Are you even halfway serious?'

'Why not?' She shrugged, trying to

sound casual while her heart thumped wildly in her chest. 'You've admitted you're tired of London. I've done enough travelling for a lifetime, and creating window displays never was my dream job. My degree is in interior design, and I'd love to get back to it.'

'But what about . . . us? I thought we'd agreed to take things slowly, not chuck in our jobs and throw in our lot together. And what about the Warrens? They're not going to let us swan in and turn their shop into some sort of Shangri-La of Cornish decorating ideas.'

'Hey, calm down.' Lila smiled. 'You asked for my thoughts, and I'm giving them to you. I didn't say we'd do it all tomorrow.' *We'll wait at least until the next day.*

'For argument's sake, say I went along with this. Where do you see the Warrens fitting in?'

'John could run the much smaller hardware side of the shop to use his experience and local knowledge. He'd have a job for as long as he wanted, but with fewer hours, and we'd share the overall responsibility.' Spelling it out crystallised her thoughts, and a surge of confidence rushed through her. This could actually work. 'Nick would be free to go to New Zealand and know his family were taken care of. Everyone wins.'

Grant frowned. 'I don't like to be a doom monger, but what if things don't work out between us? What happens to the business?'

You're coming around. I knew you would. Lila tamped down her smile and proceeded to talk sensibly about signing partnership contracts to protect everyone involved and the fact they were all adults who could rise above personal conflicts.

'What would be our first step?'

Our. You're saying our. I could hug you. 'We need to talk to Nick.'

'Your family will think you've taken leave of your senses. They'll blame me.'

'Hardly. They know me better than that.' Lila chuckled. 'No man makes me do anything I'm not one hundred percent behind.'

'I never meant to imply — '

'I know you didn't,' she conceded. 'My mom knows I've been chafing at the restrictions of my job for a while. Dad will be more wary.'

'Naturally. You're still his little girl, and he worries.' Grant held her hand, stroking her fingers. 'I'll do whatever I can to help ease his concerns.'

You're one very special man. 'I know you will.'

'If Nick thinks we've lost our marbles that'll have to be it.' His rational words brought her back to earth. 'Can you live with that?'

'Yeah. Of course.' *But I'm pretty sure I won't have to.*

'Let's go and get lunch.'

'To celebrate?'

'Yes, to celebrate.' He popped a kiss on her forehead. 'You determined woman.'

If he thought *this* was determined, he hadn't seen anything yet.

21

'The pair of you are serious, aren't you?' Nick stared from Grant to Lila and back again, shaking his head. 'Warren's Hardware becomes Cornish Coastal Designs and the byword for interior design in the county. Love has addled your brains.'

Grant didn't contradict his friend and squeezed Lila's hand, hoping she'd keep quiet for at least a few minutes. He understood Nick's reluctance, because he'd felt the same way when Lila first came up with the idea. Neither had actually used the four-letter 'L' word either, but that didn't mean it wasn't hovering in the air around them. 'If someone else had suggested this, would you still call them crazy?'

'I don't know.' Nick frowned. 'Maybe not.'

'How do you think your folks would

react if we floated the scheme to them?'
Lila jumped in. 'My guess is your
mother would love it, but John would
dig his heels in.'

'Yep, you're probably right.'

'What if someone let slip about your
job offer?' Grant interjected. 'That
person might hint that it'd be selfish of
him to hold you back. They could talk
up the plan until your dad saw it more
as freeing you, rather than giving up his
business.' He poked a bit deeper. 'And
it does benefit him. You have to see
that. Far more so than you taking over,
because he'd find it harder to step back
than he will do with us.'

Nick grinned. 'You've thought of
everything, haven't you?' He gestured
towards Lila. 'I'd no idea she was such
a devious creature. You're well and truly
sunk, mate.'

And happy to be so.

'Fine. I'll back you up. Who's going
to be the double-agent and tell on me?'

Lila's hand shot up in the air. 'That'd
better be me. I can spin the tale better.'

She slipped her coat back on. 'No time like the present. You two stay here and talk man stuff. I'm going to corner Edith and work on her before John gets home.' She glanced at her watch. 'Don't come into the house until at least seven.'

Nick's amused glance landed on Grant as he received a quick peck on the cheek along with another warning not to turn up too early. Lila ran off, slamming the door behind her.

'You do pick them, don't you?'

'From what I saw of the stunning redhead at the Lifeboat House, you might have your work cut out there too,' Grant turned the tables back around. 'Perhaps she'd enjoy an overseas adventure to New Zealand?'

'Don't be daft. I barely know her,' he mumbled.

'That's not what your dad hinted.'

'Yes, well, the man spends too long talking to tins of paint,' Nick groused.

Grant ignored him and fetched a couple of glasses and the whisky bottle from the kitchen. 'Fancy making an early start on celebrating New Year?'

'Why not. Might as well before my parents decide to disown me.'

They both knew that if anyone had a rock-solid relationship with his family, that someone was Nick. Grant's envy ran deep, but it was regret over what could have been with his own parents rather than mean-spirited.

He poured their drinks and they raised their glasses in a silent toast.

★　★　★

'New Zealand? Oh, my Lord,' Edith exclaimed. 'Fancy them wanting him to open up a new office. They must think a lot of him.' She shook her head. 'Silly boy, not wanting to tell us.'

So far so good. Over tea, because everything here happened over the tea pot, Lila had skilfully manoeuvred the conversation around to Nick. She artlessly mentioned the job offer and pretended to be shocked when Edith admitted to knowing nothing about it. 'I get the impression he's very concerned about leaving John to run the shop alone. He knows his father's health isn't what it was and that the business isn't flourishing.'

Edith's worry manifested itself in every deep line creased into her face. 'We'll have to sell up. There's no other way.'

Lila bit back a smile. She couldn't have designed a better lead-in if she'd orchestrated it herself. 'Don't be too hasty. We might come up with some way to save the business, and let Nick pursue his dream.'

'I know you're a good girl, but you're not our fairy godmother.'

Grant told me I'd waved a magic wand over his life, so maybe I could be. His confidence bolstered her and gave Lila the courage she needed to keep going. 'Listen to this and tell me if I'm simply a wacky American.' Slowly she explained her idea and then answered all of Edith's questions. Finally she leaned back in the chair and smiled. 'So, what do you think?'

John trudged into the kitchen and pulled out a chair to sit down. 'What are you women jabbering about now?'

'Tired, love?' Edith patted his arm. 'I'll pour you a cup of tea.'

He nodded, plainly too weary for conversation. Lila bided her time and waited for Edith to start the ball rolling. It didn't take long.

'We were talking about our Nick. Has he mentioned anything to you about New Zealand?'

'What about New Zealand?' John asked, plainly confused.

Edith did Lila's job for her, and ten minutes later there was no doubt she stood firmly behind the whole scheme and was ready to start convincing her reluctant husband.

'Oh, no, you're not destroying my father's business.' He glared at them both.

'So you're either going to ruin Nick's life and make him feel guilty enough to take over the shop, or you're going to drop dead working all the hours God sends.' Edith's fury bubbled over. 'I used to think you were the cleverest man I know. Maybe I should've married Philip Walker like my mum wanted.'

'Don't be like this,' he pleaded. For a second Lila almost felt sorry for him, but Edith kept going. She turned the screw tighter with a few well-placed tears and heart-rending comments about being left a widow with her only child eleven thousand miles away. The woman could give Meryl Streep a run for her money in the Oscar stakes. 'But why on earth would you and Grant be interested in working here anyway?' Edith gave him a knowing smile and John burst out laughing. 'Oh, that's the way the wind blows, is it? Can't say I'm surprised.' He reached over and patted Lila's hand. 'He's a decent chap.'

'Yeah, I know. But we're not . . . I mean there's nothing definite. This is business. But if we did somehow get together, would you mind?'

'Mind? Don't talk rubbish.'

The blunt declaration brought tears to her eyes.

'If I get the boys in here, will you at least listen to what they've got to say?' Edith persisted, giving a satisfied smile as her husband shrugged. 'Go and fetch them,' she ordered Lila.

'Will do.' She didn't wait to be asked a second time and raced out of the back door. 'Get your skates on and hurry up,' Lila yelled as she threw open the cottage door. Sprawled on the sofa and glued to the TV, both men turned and stared as if she'd gone completely mad. She launched into a garbled explanation until she finally ran out of steam. 'Are you coming or not?'

A slow smile crept across Grant's face. 'You're good.'

'She definitely is,' Nick agreed.

'Your poor father never stood a chance.'

'I'd call her an American version of Margaret Thatcher. Only much younger and prettier.'

Lila glanced down at the table. 'You've been drinking.' Her accusation only brought more smiles and good-humoured laughter.

'Only a couple of glasses to ring in the New Year,' Grant declared.

'It's only the twenty-ninth in, case you hadn't noticed.' Lila scowled, but couldn't keep it up for long. 'You're both hopeless. Pull yourselves together and come with me.'

'Yes, ma'am.' Nick sprung to his feet.

Grant came to her side, sliding his arm around her waist and pulling her to him for a quick kiss. 'We are at your command. Lead the way.'

'It's cold and starting to rain,' she warned. 'It might help clear your heads.'

'Hey, we're good, honestly,' Grant reassured her.

'Yeah, I know.' Neither man would risk something so important to them all. 'Let's go.'

* * *

'What do you think, John?' Grant asked the big question. They'd talked back and forth for a couple of hours, fuelled by more cups of tea and slabs of Christmas cake. 'It's early days, and there's a lot to think about and plan, but I reckon we could be open in some form by Easter in time for tourist season.'

'When would you go, Nick?' John made an effort to smile, but Grant caught the tremor in his voice. He'd lost one child, and now the other wanted to move to the other side of the world.

'If I give them my answer next week, it'll take a while to sort out work visas, and the office is still being built, so I'm guessing maybe early March,' Nick ventured. 'It'd only be a two-year contract initially, and with the increased pay I can afford to come home several times.'

John nodded. 'Fair enough.' He patted Edith's hand. 'I know this dear woman's worried about me. Losing

Belle . . . it tore me up, and I haven't been the same since. Never will be.' He glanced around the table at them all. 'I'm not going to pretend I *want* to agree to all this, but it makes sense.'

A brief frisson of panic ran through Grant. He knew nothing of interior design beyond his carpentry. Lila had been in Cornwall for a grand total of eight days. John wasn't exactly one hundred percent invested in the scheme.

'We're goin' to be fine,' Lila whispered. 'One step at a time. It's no different from when you're building a piece of furniture.'

'I don't know about you lot, but I'm starving,' John announced. 'What've we got to eat?'

'Nothing much. All this hullabaloo threw me all off,' Edith grumbled. 'The chops should've been in cooking before now.'

Lila's eyes sparkled. 'I suggest we go out and celebrate. We'll get dinner and toast Cornish Coastal Designs and Nick's Kiwi adventure.'

Grant watched in amusement as she swept everyone up in her enthusiasm so that five minutes later they were all walking down the hill together into Port Carne. The back-and-forth argument about where to eat ended up with Nick and John tossing a coin.

'Heads, I win. The Lifeboat House it is,' Nick proclaimed, grinning broadly.

Grant tapped Lila's shoulder. 'No matchmaking. Stay out of it. Remember, he's going eleven thousand miles away to work.'

'So what?' The flecks of gold in her eyes intensified. 'Since when did a little distance stop anyone who knew what they wanted?'

Suddenly they weren't talking about Nick and the gorgeous Emma any longer, and his breath caught in his throat. 'I can't imagine.'

'Didn't think so.' Lila brushed a soft kiss on his cheek and ran off laughing to catch up with Nick, who'd strode out in front, obviously keen to get to the restaurant.

He'd leave his old friend to his fate. Lila unleashed was one unstoppable force.

22

Lila strolled into the cottage without bothering to knock. 'Edith sent me with a cottage pie, whatever that is, for us to have later. She didn't mind us eating on our own tonight.' She set down the glass dish on the kitchen counter and took off the snowy white cloth to take a look.

'It's minced beef and onion topped with mashed potato.' Grant draped his arm around her shoulder. 'It'll be good. Sit down and tell me how your calls went.' He encouraged her over to the sofa and tucked her in beside him.

'I've burned my bridges. I quit my job and then called my folks.' She grinned. 'That went pretty much as we predicted. I told them I'd be coming home next week to talk it over some more and get my things sorted out.'

'I'll miss you,' he confessed, 'but I

'know you need to go.'

'Next time you'll come with me.' Lila wondered if she'd been too blunt, but Grant's face broke into a broad smile. 'It's been a heck of a twenty-four hours.'

'Certainly has.'

Since yesterday, they'd talked out some of the financial details of the partnership and got a rough plan drawn up to renovate the shop. Lila's to-do list was a mile long, but she'd always thrived on a challenge. 'How's Nick today?'

Grant laughed. 'Bemused by everything happening so fast. You stirred things up when you put a word in Emma's ear. I admit I was wrong.'

'Did I hear you right?' Lila pretended to clean out her ears. 'Can you repeat that?'

'No.' He dived in and tickled her, refusing to stop until she begged for mercy. 'They're going out for dinner tonight. Luckily it's her night off.'

'There's no luck about it.' She smirked. 'But how — '

'I told her she didn't have much time

to waste and needed to make things happen pronto.'

Grant's disbelief showed in his eyes. 'You're one crazy lady.'

'I'll take that as a compliment.'

His phone suddenly beeped. 'Why on earth is Edith texting me? I didn't even realise she knew how.' He scanned over the message and frowned.

'What's wrong?'

'I'm not sure. She says I've got a visitor and I need to come to the house.'

'Why doesn't she send them up here?'

'No clue.' He dragged himself up from the sofa and held out his hand. 'Come on.'

'You sure?'

'Of course I am.'

The natural way they'd eased into being together still caught Lila unawares sometimes. 'It's probably nothing serious. Edith enjoys playing with the new phone Nick gave her for Christmas.'

'I'm sure you're right. You usually are,' he teased.

★ ★ ★

'Dad?' Grant stared at the shabby grey-haired man hunched over at the kitchen table.

'Isn't this a treat?' Edith threw him an anxious look. 'Your dad travelled all the way from Edinburgh today to spend the New Year with us.'

'Wonderful.' His brain whirred with possible scenarios for his father's sudden appearance, most of them bad.

'I told this dear lady that I'd booked a room at the pub, but she insisted I ring and cancel.'

'We've got an empty bedroom, so it's silly to waste your money,' Edith declared. 'I'm going to pop down to the shop for another pint of milk so we don't run short.'

'I'll do it,' Lila offered.

'Thanks, love, but you stay here.' She gathered her handbag and coat and hurried off.

From the little Grant had shared with the family here, Edith knew something of his difficult relationship with his father and had realised he needed Lila by his side. Grant got the introductions over with, and Lila launched into her typical charm offensive. Soon Ian was chatting away as though he'd known her forever.

'Grant, why don't you and your dad go into the other room where it's more comfortable? I'll fix us a hot drink. What would you prefer?' Lila turned back to Ian.

'Black coffee, please.'

'Go on.' She shooed Grant away. 'I know you want tea.'

The two men sat on opposite ends of the sofa and didn't say anything for a minute. Before Grant could ask his father what was going on, Ian beat him to it.

'I got my test results yesterday afternoon and I wanted to come and tell you myself.'

'Is everything okay?' They might not be close, but the idea of losing his father prematurely left him numb.

There was too much unsaid between them.

'I'm not A1, but I should be around to pester you for a few more years unless I get run over by a bus tomorrow.' Ian's black humour forced a reluctant smile out of Grant. 'I've got to have regular check-ups and take tablets the rest of my life, but it could be worse.' He grimaced. 'Much worse.'

Grant hugged his father. 'That's great news.'

'I thought so too.' Ian's raspy voice betrayed his emotions. 'You can let go of me now. I'm not planning to croak anytime soon.'

Lila came in and set a tray down on the table. 'Here we are. Is everything all right?'

'It certainly is.' Grant couldn't stop grinning. 'Dad's got the almost-all clear. Nothing life-threatening.'

'Oh, that's wonderful news, Mr. Hawkins.'

'Call me Ian, my dear,' he suggested. 'I suspect we'll be seeing a lot more of each other in the future.'

Grant couldn't ever remember seeing his father this happy.

'I sure hope so. Now, I'm going to sit next to you so you can tell me what this renegade got up to as a little boy.' Lila perched on the cushion next to him.

Grant allowed their chatter to pleasantly wash over him. The stories his father told about his childhood stirred up a lot of good memories, reminding him it hadn't been nonstop sadness.

'He still watches *Coronation Street*, you know,' Lila said.

'I can believe it. He loved that nonsense.' Ian laughed at Lila's comment before falling quiet.

'I want to be able to talk about Mum,' Grant murmured. 'I need to.'

'I know, son.' Ian sighed. 'And we must talk about your Belle too. I wish I'd known her better.'

Lila smiled. 'She was such a beautiful person, and one of my best friends.'

'That must help you.' He nodded towards Grant. 'Less explaining to do. I'm glad

246

you aren't copying my mistakes.'

One day Grant planned to share how close he'd come to doing exactly that before a beautiful woman with hazel eyes, a soft drawl, and a softer heart turned his life upside down. For now he'd simply appreciate his good fortune.

Ian sipped his coffee. 'How do the Cornish ring in the New Year?'

'Well, St. Ives and Newquay are the party hot spots, but Belle and I always stayed here in Port Carne,' Grant said. 'They set off fireworks over the harbour and all the restaurants and pubs stay open late. There'll be live music, and lots of people wear fancy dress.'

'Did Belle?' Lila asked.

'Of course. Did you ever know her to turn down the chance of dressing up?'

'Nope. I bet she made you join in too.'

Grant rolled his eyes. 'Beauty and the Beast was her favourite, but one year we did Laurel and Hardy.' For a few seconds his mind drifted away, and only

Lila's hand on his arm brought him back.

'Sounds like a good evening.' Ian yawned. 'The long day is catching up on me. I'm ready for bed.'

'Why don't you stay out in the cottage with me instead? You can have my bed and I'll make do with the sofa.' Grant couldn't vocalise how much he wanted to make the most of this time together. 'Please.'

'Thanks. I'd be happy to.'

'I'll get your luggage.'

'I've only got one small duffle bag.'

'Doesn't matter.' Grant's insistence made his father smile.

'Don't worry about Edith,' Lila chimed in. 'I'll tell her about the change of plans when she gets back, and we'll see you both in the morning.'

'You're a star,' Grant said.

'You're welcome.' Her glorious smile lit him up from the inside out. 'Anyway, if I hang around here, I can wheedle more mince pies out of Edith. I'm not dumb.'

You certainly aren't.

'Remember you've still got the cottage pie to warm up if you're hungry.'

'She's telling us to go, son. Get the hint.' Ian interrupted. 'Give the lady a goodnight kiss, and I'll meet you in the kitchen.' He left them alone.

'Are you going to follow your father's orders?'

Grant folded his arms and studied her for a moment. 'Which part? The going bit, or the kiss?'

'Both. But in the right order.'

'And what would that be, pretty lady?'

Lila's contagious laughter filled the room. 'The kiss will be pretty difficult to achieve if you go first, smart mouth.'

He held out his hand. 'Come here. I'll show you who's smart.' Lila stepped closer and he wrapped his arms around her. 'Tell me if this works.' He drew them into a deep, wonderful kiss, and for several magical moments lost himself in her sweetness. 'Well?'

'Perfect,' she sighed, and it took all his self-control not to kiss her again. 'Your father's waiting.'

Grant nodded. 'Come and join us for breakfast. Please.' He teased a strand of silky hair that'd come loose from her ponytail.

'I'll be there.' She murmured something under her breath, but he couldn't catch what she said.

'What was that?'

Lila's cheeks burned. 'Something I shouldn't have said. Not yet.'

'We promised each other honesty. Come on.'

A flash of defiance made her eyes gleam. 'Okay. You asked for it. Don't blame me if it freaks you out. I said I'll always be there if you want me.'

'Oh, Lila.' Grant's throat tightened. Before he could reply, the sound of the front door slamming echoed through the house. 'Tomorrow — we'll talk then,' he whispered seconds before the door burst open and Edith bustled back in, red-faced and out of breath.

'It's some busy down in the street. I got the last pint of milk in the shop. Is everything all right?'

Lila swiftly told Edith what'd gone on in her absence while Grant struggled to get his emotions under control. He wasn't sure he'd get through New Year's Eve if things got any more of a challenge.

23

Lila leaned on the harbour wall and relished the beautiful, bright, cloudless day. People kept telling her that this time of year would usually be damp and chilly, but on principle she refused to believe them. After breakfast, she'd hung around John in the shop to fine-tune her ideas before bringing her sketchbook and pencils down here. She'd staked her claim on a bench set in a sheltered spot on the way to the outer quay and got to work. It'd proved to be perfect for drafting her first ideas for the Cornish Coastal Designs line. The famous striped Cornish Blue pottery and the ever-changing colours of the sea and surrounding coastline all inspired her. It'd been years since she'd experienced this level of excitement, and it brought back the reasons why she'd chosen to study interior design in the first place.

'Sneaking out on me already? We missed you at lunch.'

Grant's deep voice made her jump and she dropped her bag, watching in horror as the pencils rolled out and her papers scattered all over the cobblestones. 'Don't let them blow away,' she screamed.

He rushed to pick everything up and returned it safely to her, then launched into a barrage of apologies. She stopped him with a strategic kiss just before he would've started all over again.

'I get the hint.' He grinned. 'What have you been up to?'

'Sit down and I'll tell you.'

'By the way, I haven't forgotten.' Grant's quietly spoken words surprised her because, she'd expected him to delay any restart of last night's abandoned conversation.

'Good.' She nodded. 'First I'll run through all this with you while it's fresh in my mind.' She slid her hand through his arm and steered them over to her new favourite bench. He didn't make any comment as she showed him everything, and a niggle of worry edged into her brain.

'You're a genius. I've never been much for the overly nautical look, but this captures the environment perfectly. Cornwall doesn't suit the bright, crisp Mediterranean colours you often see used in seaside places.'

Lila breathed again. 'You scared me there for a minute. You were so quiet I thought you must hate it.'

'Sorry. Belle often complained about that too. She claimed she never knew what I was thinking.' His brooding eyes rested on her and she sensed a deep insecurity behind his words.

'I am *not* complaining, so get that out of your head right now. I've got to get used to your ways, and you need to do the same for me in return. That's all. It takes time.' She rested her head on his shoulder. 'Just so you know, I don't intend to give up. You're stuck with me.'

'Thank heavens.' Grant's voice faltered. 'Last night you said you'd always be there if I wanted you.'

'I meant it.'

'Good, because I do.'

A surge of joy filled her heart.

'I'm trying to be sensible. To give you time to weigh your options. You need to talk to your family and mull it over with them. These are huge decisions.'

'But?'

A shy smile tugged at his mouth. 'What makes you think there's one of those?'

'I heard it.' Lila touched his forehead. 'Up here.'

'Do you have a solution, genius woman?'

She caught the thread of worry behind his half-joking words. 'I don't think love necessarily precludes being sensible and making wise decisions.'

'Love. Are you . . . '

'Yes. I'm sure. I'm not a teenager. I've had crushes before, and this isn't one.' She hurried on before he could interrupt. 'I know you've been in love before, but that doesn't bother me.

You've got a big heart. There's plenty for me.'

'It's yours.'

His simple declaration brought tears to her eyes. 'And mine belongs to you too.'

Grant wrapped his arms around her in a warm embrace. 'We'll do all the sensible things. But in here — ' His hand rested over her heart. ' — we'll know.'

'That works for me.'

'Good. Let's get ready to see in the New Year.'

⋆　⋆　⋆

'You want me to put those on?' Grant frowned and took the heavy yellow oilskins from Lila's outstretched hands. 'Why?'

'Add a pair of galoshes and a fisherman-style jumper underneath. Meet me back here in ten minutes. I'm going to change.'

'Dare I ask what into?'

'You can ask, but I'm not going to

tell you,' she teased, and ran off upstairs.

Ian strolled in, holding a mug of coffee. 'She's got you wondering. The best women always do that.'

'Did Mum play the same trick on you?'

A wistful smile creased his father's face. 'She certainly did. Kept me on my toes.' He pointed to the clothes in Grant's hands. 'You'd better hurry.'

Throughout the day, Grant had discovered more about his parents than he'd ever known, and his father's habitual reticence gradually eased as he opened up. There'd been no lightning bolt, rather the steady realisation that they weren't as far apart as they'd always believed themselves to be. The knowledge emboldened Grant now.

'You're coming with us tonight, I hope?'

Ian held up his hand. 'No, but don't start on me. I'll come along later with Edith and John. She told me they take folding chairs down to sit on the quay and watch the fireworks. That'll suit me better. I can't stand around all those hours.'

'Sorry, I didn't think. I just wanted — '

'I know, and I appreciate it. We'll all be together at midnight and see in the New Year together.'

Grant nodded and left to do Lila's bidding.

'Cover your eyes,' she called. He heard light footsteps on the stairs. 'Okay. You can look now.'

As Grant turned, he sucked in a deep breath. A halo of dark silky hair fanned out over her shoulders, and exotic silver make-up lit up her eyes and lips. Lila's body was encased in a pale blue mermaid costume, and the silver scales twinkled in the light. The tail fanned out near her ankles, and her feet sported a pair of sparkly silver flip-flops.

'You'll be cold.'

'I'm relying on you to keep me warm. You're the doomed fisherman I've lured onto the rocks. My wish is your command now.' Lila's entrancing soft drawl wrapped around him and he was well and truly lost. 'Come on. Let's go and get this party started.'

'Can you walk in that?' Ever practical, he couldn't see how she'd manage.

'Of course. I'm a woman. We can do anything.' Her smile broadened. 'And if I get tired, you'll carry me. You've done that before.'

'Lorelei. The original siren mermaid. Very appropriate.'

'I thought so.'

'Let's go and amaze Port Carne with my catch.' Grant laughed and tucked her arm through his.

* * *

Lila wriggled in Grant's arms and wished she'd dressed him in something cosier to snuggle into than cold, slick oilskins. She briefly thought of Nashville and the crowds getting ready to bring in the New Year there later. The first burst of fireworks soared into the sky, and the people thronging the harbour area let out a rousing cheer. They'd staked out a good spot for their group and were all together now. Nick had managed to drag Emma away from work, and they were leaning back against the wall behind his parents and Ian.

'I almost didn't come to Cornwall for Christmas, and I definitely didn't intend to stay for New Year,' Grant mused.

'Glad you did?'

'Understatement of the year.'

Lila grinned. 'Yeah, isn't it?'

A shower of red rockets filled the sky, appearing to set fire to the tiny boats bobbing around in the water, and an approving roar went up from the crowd.

'The big finale is coming up,' Grant said, tightening his hold on her.

As the night erupted with a splash of gold, the church bells began to ring, and everyone counted down the chimes.

'Happy New Year!' Grant shouted, seizing Lila in a passionate kiss. 'I love you, Lila Caswell.'

'I love you too. Happy New Year.'

They broke apart to join in the celebrations, knowing that when tonight was over, this was only the beginning for them.

24

One Year Later

'Wow! We made the front cover of *Cornish Craft*.' Lila brandished the glossy magazine in Grant's face. 'Listen to this. 'The place to go for all the best in Cornish design — Cornish Coastal Designs is a must-see for anyone interested in reflecting the uniqueness of the county in their home.' '

'I always said you were a genius, but you didn't believe me.'

'It's not just me. We've done this together. The three of us.' She pointed at John, busy chatting to a customer. 'He's been a big hit because people enjoy talking to a genuine local, especially foreigners like me or those from the far-away wilds of Devon,' Lila teased. 'And whose unique furniture is featured in one of the pictures they printed?'

Grant swept into a deep bow. 'I succumb to your superior intellect, Mrs. Hawkins.'

Her cheeks heated and she twirled the gold ring gracing her left hand. The novelty of being married still made her act all girlish at times, but after only four months that didn't strike her as unreasonable.

John came over to join them. 'So you should. She's a smart one. I thought you were both mad, but you've proved me wrong. I've even taken a holiday for the first time in thirty years, so I couldn't be happier.'

'And your wife is too, so it's all good.' Lila kept Edith's new plan for them taking a cruise in the spring to herself.

Nick strolled in. 'Aren't you closed yet? It's time to get ready to see in another New Year.'

'Is Emma joining us?'

'Of course. She can't resist being seen around with the only handsome young man with a genuine tan in the middle of your winter.' He flexed his arm muscles in the short-sleeved shirt he'd persisted in wearing despite the cold weather.

'You vain creature,' Lila teased. The romance she'd kick-started was flourishing. Thanks to the wonders of modern technology, the couple had 'dated' long-distance since Nick flew out to New Zealand at Easter. He'd been back now for three weeks and hadn't let the grass grow under his feet. The last thing Lila heard, he'd almost convinced Emma to visit him in the spring.

'Are you pair dressing up tonight?'

She shook her head. 'We decided to give it a miss. We've been too busy to find any costumes. Despite the fact that half of the shops are still closed for the winter, we've been slammed over the holidays.' She smiled. 'Nick, would you mind helping your dad to close up? I want my husband to myself for a while before the evening kicks off.'

'No problem.'

By Grant's curious expression, he

guessed she was up to something. 'I'd better do what I'm told,' he grunted.

'That's what the best husbands do, so I'm told,' Nick jested.

John playfully jabbed his son's arm. 'You'll find out soon enough.'

'Where are we going?' Grant asked.

'For a walk.'

He grimaced. 'We won't be standing out in the cold long enough later?'

'Don't argue.' Lila had been trying to get him alone all day. She unhitched her new red wool coat from the pegs by the door and slipped it on. 'Come on, Mr. Hawkins.'

'Yes, ma'am.' Grant's attempt at a southern drawl made her laugh. Ever since they'd got married in Nashville, he couldn't resist trying to sound like his newly acquired relatives. 'You'll ruin those if we go to the beach.' He pointed to her flimsy red shoes.

Lila emptied out a plastic carrier bag, and two pairs of boots fell out onto the floor. 'Galoshes. Yours and mine. Any other dumb questions?'

'I wouldn't dare.' He changed out of his own brown loafers. 'Let's go.' He seized her hand and hurried her out of the shop. She was unusually quiet all the way down, and he gave up trying to get any conversation out of her. She'd tell him what was bothering her soon enough.

They reached the beach, but instead of heading down to walk along by the sea, Lila steered them over to Belle's memorial.

'What's on your mind, love?' Grant asked, and pulled her to him, wrapping his arms tightly around her.

'I've been thinking a lot about Belle recently.'

'Any particular reason?' Lila didn't answer right away and glanced down, toeing the sand with her boot. 'What's wrong? Tell me.' He grasped her shoulders, forcing her to look at him.

'Nothing's wrong. In fact everything's right, but . . . ' Tears glazed her eyes.

'You can share anything with me. You know that.'

'I'm so very happy.' A tear rolled

down her cheek. 'I love being married to you, and I know you're happy too. Do we deserve it?'

He wasn't sure how to respond. 'Does anyone?'

'But Belle wanted a child with you so badly,' she suddenly blurted out. 'I know she did. And I know the reasons why it didn't happen, but I can't stop feeling guilty . . . '

Grant's heart raced. 'Are you trying to tell me we're having a baby?' The second she nodded, he lifted her off her feet and swept her into the air. 'Oh my God, that's wonderful.'

'It is, isn't it?' Lila laughed. 'It really is.'

Very gently, he set her back down on the sand. 'I do understand. I'm not totally insensitive.'

'How do you feel about it?'

'Mixed. I'm not going to pretend otherwise.' He sighed. 'I often disappointed Belle. I had too many hang-ups from my childhood between losing my mum so young and Dad not knowing how to handle me.'

'That wasn't your fault.'

'No, but it wasn't Belle's either.' He needed to acknowledge his failings. 'You know I could have done more to make things better for her.' His tension eased as she rested her head on his chest. 'But the thing is, we could fret nonstop, and in the end it simply is what it is. You know Belle was never a woman for what-ifs. I can't change what happened and neither can you. I honestly believe it'd please her to see I've become a stronger person. I'm not going to spoil what we have by always looking back, and I'm sure she wouldn't want me to.'

'You're totally right, and maybe I just needed to hear you say it,' Lila admitted.

'I hope that's one thing I'm better at now, thanks to you.'

'You sure are.'

Grant drew her into a soft, lingering kiss. 'Are you going to let me into the secret of when I'm going to be a father?'

'Late July.' Lila beamed. 'If you'd like, we can tell everyone tonight.'

'If I like? I want to shout it from the rooftops.' His unbridled enthusiasm warmed her all the way through her body. 'My dad will be thrilled. I'm really glad he came down for the holidays.' He smiled. 'This will be the best New Year ever.'

Grant let go of her for a moment and walked over to the wall to rest his hand on Belle's name. With a broad smile, he turned back to Lila and held out his hand. 'Let's go. It's time to start the celebrations.'

THE DOCTOR'S DAUGHTER

Sharon Booth

After the death of her father, who had been the trusted GP of their little Yorkshire village of Bramblewick, Anna Gray decides to accept her childhood sweetheart Ben's proposal of marriage, leave her position as receptionist at the practice, and move to Kent. There's nothing to hold her here . . . is there? When Connor Blake, the new GP, arrives, along with his extraordinary but troubled daughter Gracie, Anna begins to have doubts. But how can that possibly be, when she and Ben are the perfect couple? Or, at least, so everybody says . . .

CROSSING WITH THE CAPTAIN

Judy Jarvie

Ten years ago, Libby Grant and Drew Muldoon dated for six months. Despite a string of disasters, they became engaged — then Libby broke up by letter while Drew was at sea. Now on a leisure cruise around Spain and Italy, she discovers to her horror that Drew is the captain of the ship. Can they work through their past problems and rekindle the spark and hope of their old relationship? Or will the mysterious thefts and hacking incidents on board the ship throw a serious spanner in the works?

THE LEMON TREE

Sheila Spencer-Smith

When her boyfriend Charles suggests they spend two months apart, Zoe's brother Simon invites her to come stay with him and his wife Thea in the idyllic village of Elounda on Crete, where they run a taverna. There Zoe meets Adam, an English tour guide. But business at the taverna isn't exactly brisk, and Adam will be leaving soon. Can Zoe make things work, or will she decide to return to her old life and Charles?

THE RECLUSIVE DUKE

Fenella J. Miller

When Lydia Sinclair is left to care for her orphaned nieces and nephews, she discovers they are distant relatives of the Duke of Hemingford. She sets off to his estate, children in tow, determined to persuade him to assume responsibility for his cousins. But the duke refuses to have these unwanted relatives foisted upon him. However, his man of business compassionately installs the new arrivals in the nearby Dower House. Will the duke evict them when he discovers this deception?